THE ROCKING-DEAD

By Dana Sullivan

RED CHAIR
·PRESS·

Egremont, Massachusetts

Dead Max Comix is produced and published by:
Red Chair Press PO Box 333 South Egremont, MA 01258-0333
www.redchairpress.com

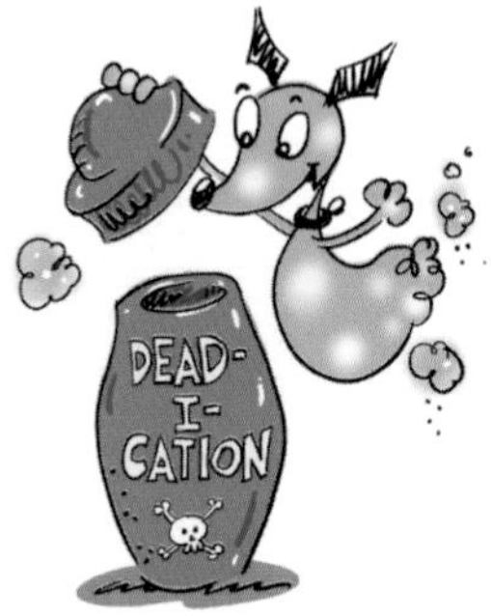
DEAD-
I-
CATION

To all my dogs and teachers,
Thanks for sticking with me.
–Dana

Publisher's Cataloging-In-Publication Data
Names: Sullivan, Dana, 1958- author, illustrator.

Title: The rocking dead / by Dana Sullivan.

Description: Egremont, Massachusetts : Red Chair Press, [2020] | Series: Dead Max comix ; book 2 | Interest age level: 009-013. | Summary: "Derrick and Doug should have asked for advice before they started a band without inviting Kim and Keisha to join. To get even, Kim challenges the guys to come up with awesome costumes for Comic-Con AND enter the upcoming Battle of the Bands. There's only one problem: Derrick and Doug's band stinks and they know the girls' new band is going to smoke them. Meanwhile, the kids go to the animal shelter ... and end up falling in ... love. How can they find homes for all the critters? Will the Battle of the Bands mean the end of Derrick and Kim?"--Provided by publisher.

Identifiers: ISBN 9781634408585 (library hardcover) | ISBN 9781634408592 (paperback) | ISBN 9781634408608 (ebook PDF)

Subjects: LCSH: Middle school students--Comic books, strips, etc. | Rock groups--Competitions--Comic books, strips, etc. | Animal shelters--Comic books, strips, etc. | Spirits--Comic books, strips, etc. | CYAC: Middle school students--Cartoons and comics. | Rock groups--Competitions--Cartoons and comics. | Animal shelters--Cartoons and comics. | Spirits--Cartoons and comics. | LCGFT: Graphic novels.

Classification: LCC PZ7.7 .S852 2020 (print) | LCC PZ7.7 (ebook) | DDC 741.5973 [Fic]--dc23

LC record available at https://lccn.loc.gov/2019953594

Printed in the United States of America

04 1P CGBF20

CAULDRON ~~TABLE~~ OF CONTENTS

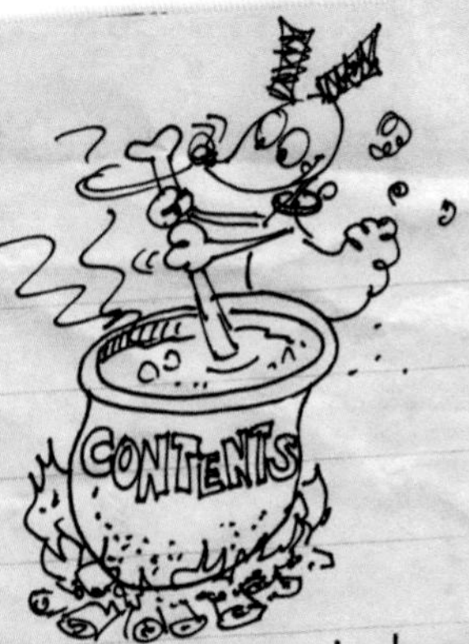

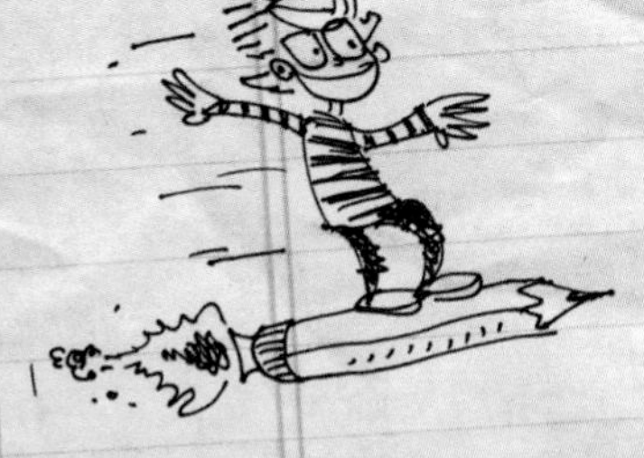

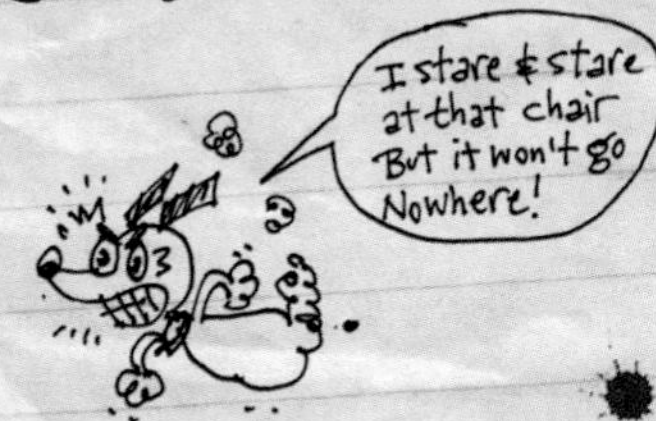

I stare & stare at that chair But it won't go Nowhere!

RED CHAIR PRESS

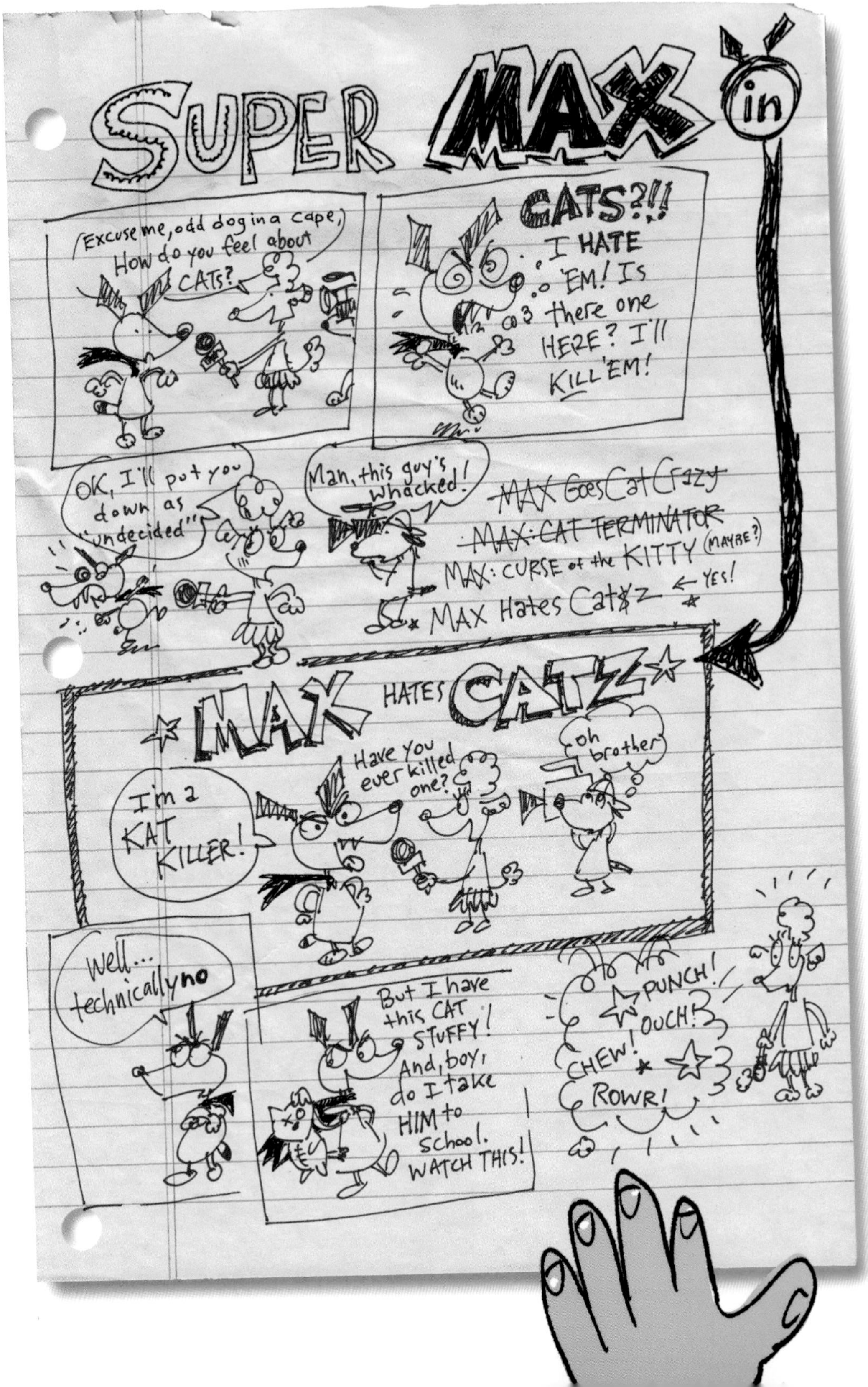

SUPER MAX in
Excuse me, odd dog in a cape, How do you feel about CATS?
CATS?!! I HATE 'EM! Is there one HERE? I'll KILL 'EM!
OK, I'll put you down as "undecided"
Man, this guy's whacked!
MAX Goes Cat Crazy
MAX: CAT TERMINATOR
MAX: CURSE of the KITTY (MAYBE?)
MAX Hates Catz ← YES!
MAX HATES CATZ
Have you ever killed one?
oh brother
I'm a KAT KILLER!
Well... technically no
But I have this CAT STUFFY! And, boy, do I take HIM to school. WATCH THIS!
PUNCH! OUCH! CHEW! ROWR!

And how do you feel about RATZ?
ZOUNDS! I like YOU just FINE!
Hmm
ESPECIALLY if you made me a cool Canine CAR!
PAWSOME!
MAX
That MAX is a CAT-TASTROPHE!
VROOOOOM!
He's a FOE to FELINES!
ME-OUCH!
SHAR-PEI
get the Lead out, cats!
Lookin' Sharp!

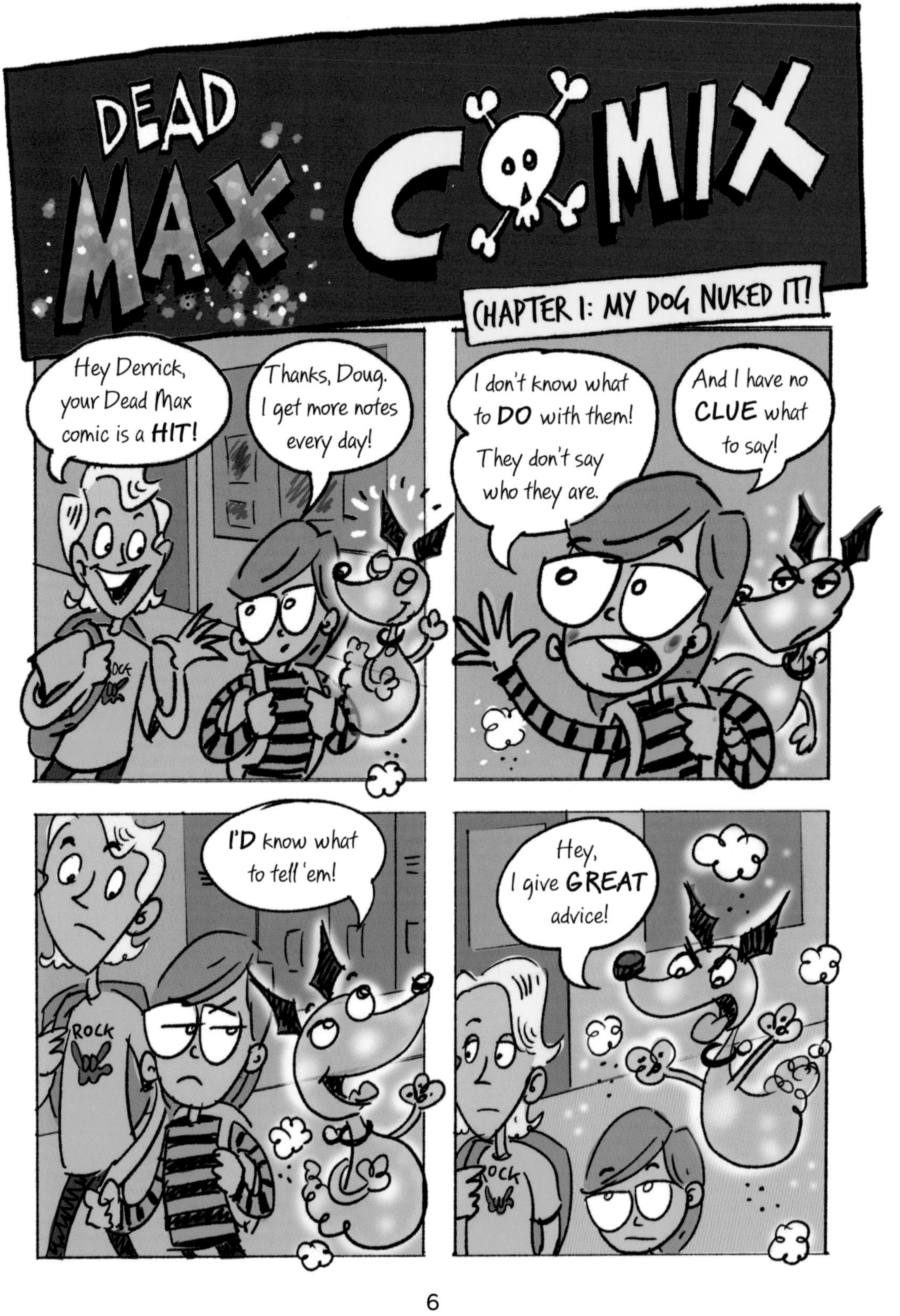
DEAD MAX COMIX
CHAPTER 1: MY DOG NUKED IT!
Hey Derrick, your Dead Max comic is a HIT!
Thanks, Doug. I get more notes every day!
I don't know what to DO with them!
They don't say who they are.
And I have no CLUE what to say!
I'D know what to tell 'em!
Hey, I give GREAT advice!

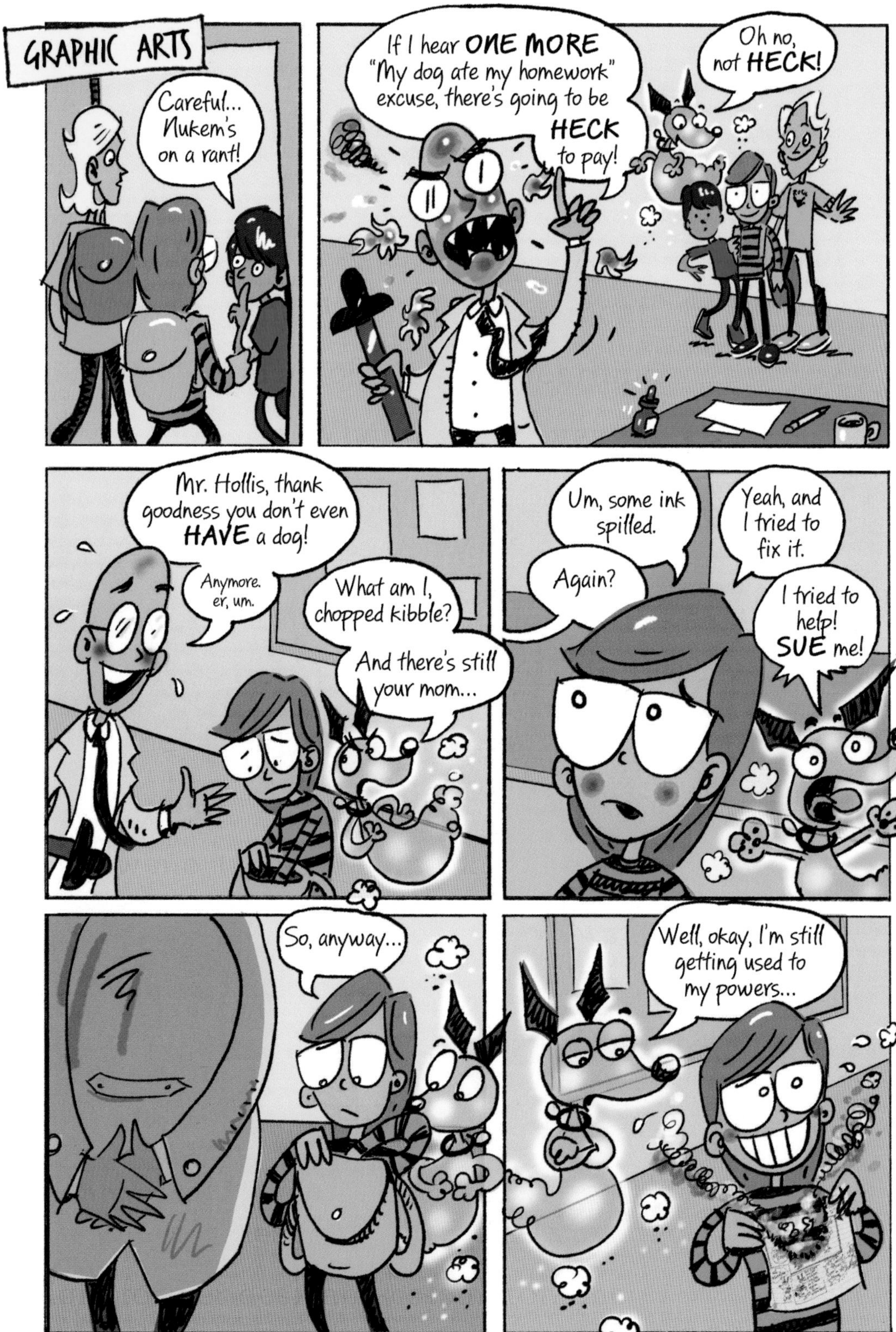
GRAPHIC ARTS
Careful... Nukem's on a rant!
If I hear ONE MORE "My dog ate my homework" excuse, there's going to be HECK to pay!
Oh no, not HECK!
Mr. Hollis, thank goodness you don't even HAVE a dog!
Anymore. er, um.
What am I, chopped kibble?
And there's still your mom...
Um, some ink spilled.
Again?
Yeah, and I tried to fix it.
I tried to help! SUE me!
So, anyway...
Well, okay, I'm still getting used to my powers...

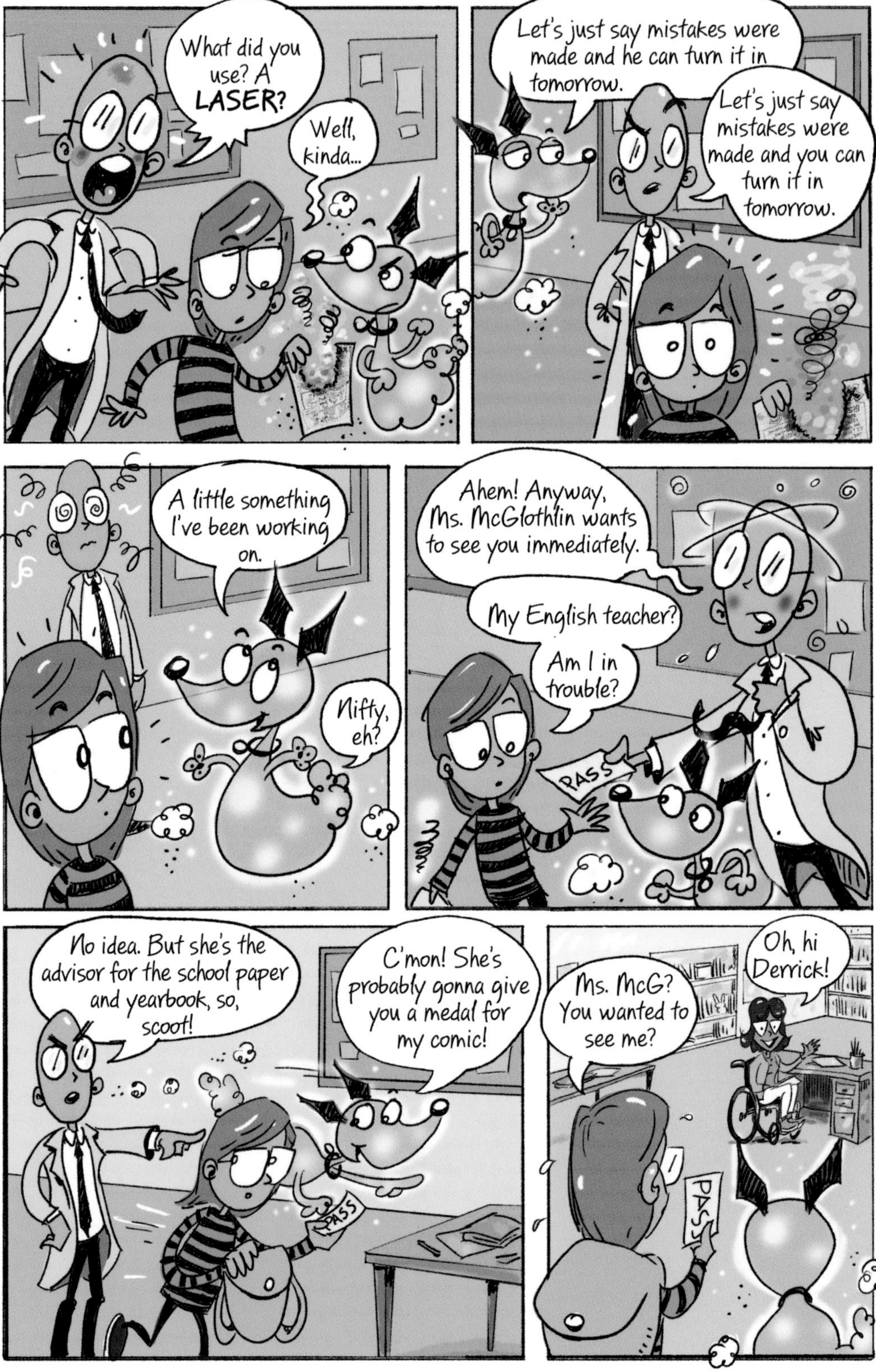

What did you use? A LASER?
Well, kinda...
Let's just say mistakes were made and he can turn it in tomorrow.
Let's just say mistakes were made and you can turn it in tomorrow.
A little something I've been working on.
Nifty, eh?
Ahem! Anyway, Ms. McGlothlin wants to see you immediately.
My English teacher?
Am I in trouble?
PASS
No idea. But she's the advisor for the school paper and yearbook, so, scoot!
C'mon! She's probably gonna give you a medal for my comic!
PASS
Ms. McG? You wanted to see me?
Oh, hi Derrick!
PASS

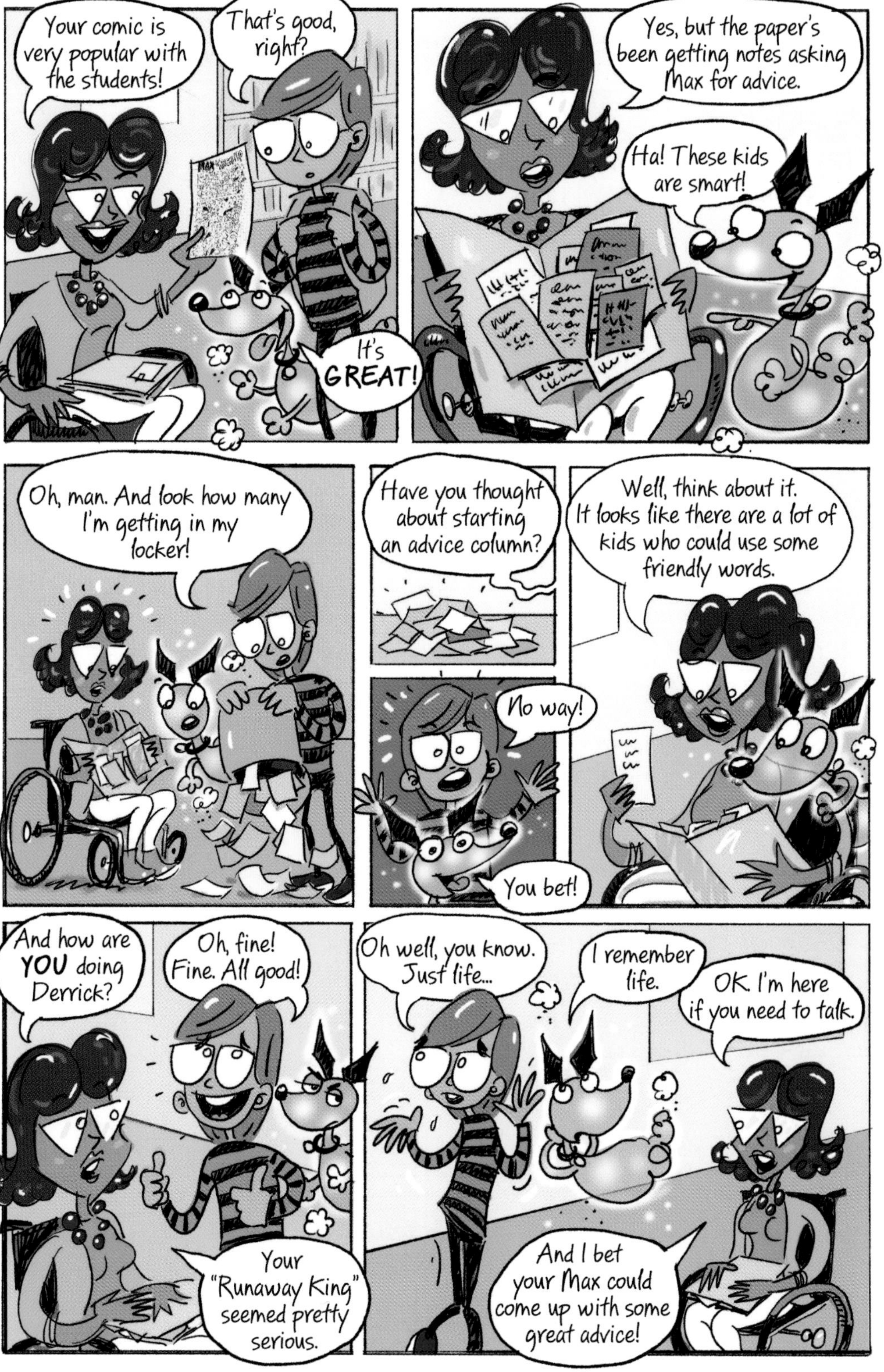
Your comic is very popular with the students!
That's good, right?
It's GREAT!
Yes, but the paper's been getting notes asking Max for advice.
Ha! These kids are smart!
Oh, man. And look how many I'm getting in my locker!
Have you thought about starting an advice column?
No way!
You bet!
Well, think about it. It looks like there are a lot of kids who could use some friendly words.
And how are YOU doing Derrick?
Oh, fine! Fine. All good!
Your "Runaway King" seemed pretty serious.
Oh well, you know. Just life...
I remember life.
OK. I'm here if you need to talk.
And I bet your Max could come up with some great advice!

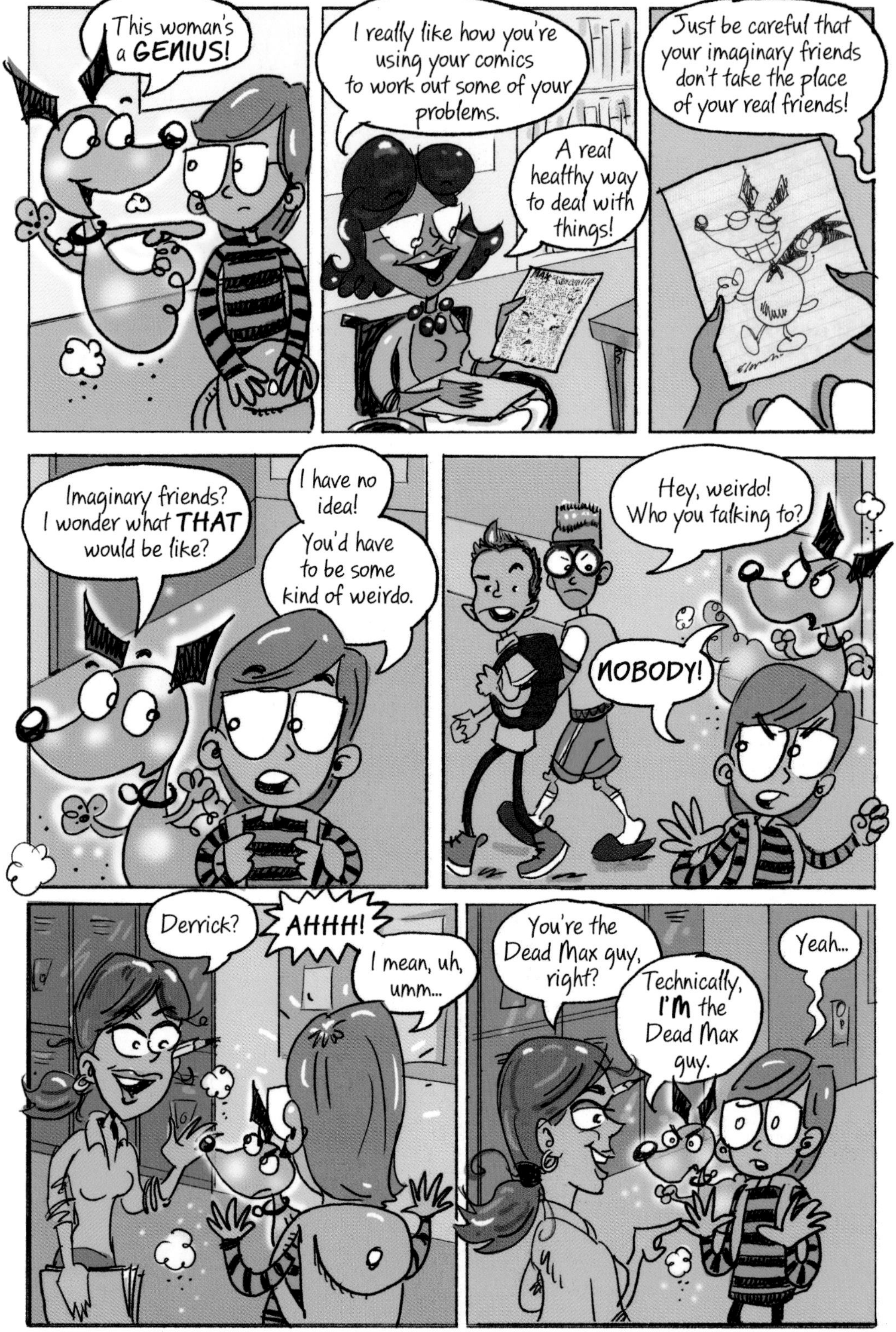
This woman's a GENIUS!
I really like how you're using your comics to work out some of your problems.
A real healthy way to deal with things!
Just be careful that your imaginary friends don't take the place of your real friends!
Imaginary friends? I wonder what THAT would be like?
I have no idea!
You'd have to be some kind of weirdo.
Hey, weirdo! Who you talking to?
NOBODY!
Derrick?
AHHH!
I mean, uh, umm...
You're the Dead Max guy, right?
Technically, I'M the Dead Max guy.
Yeah...

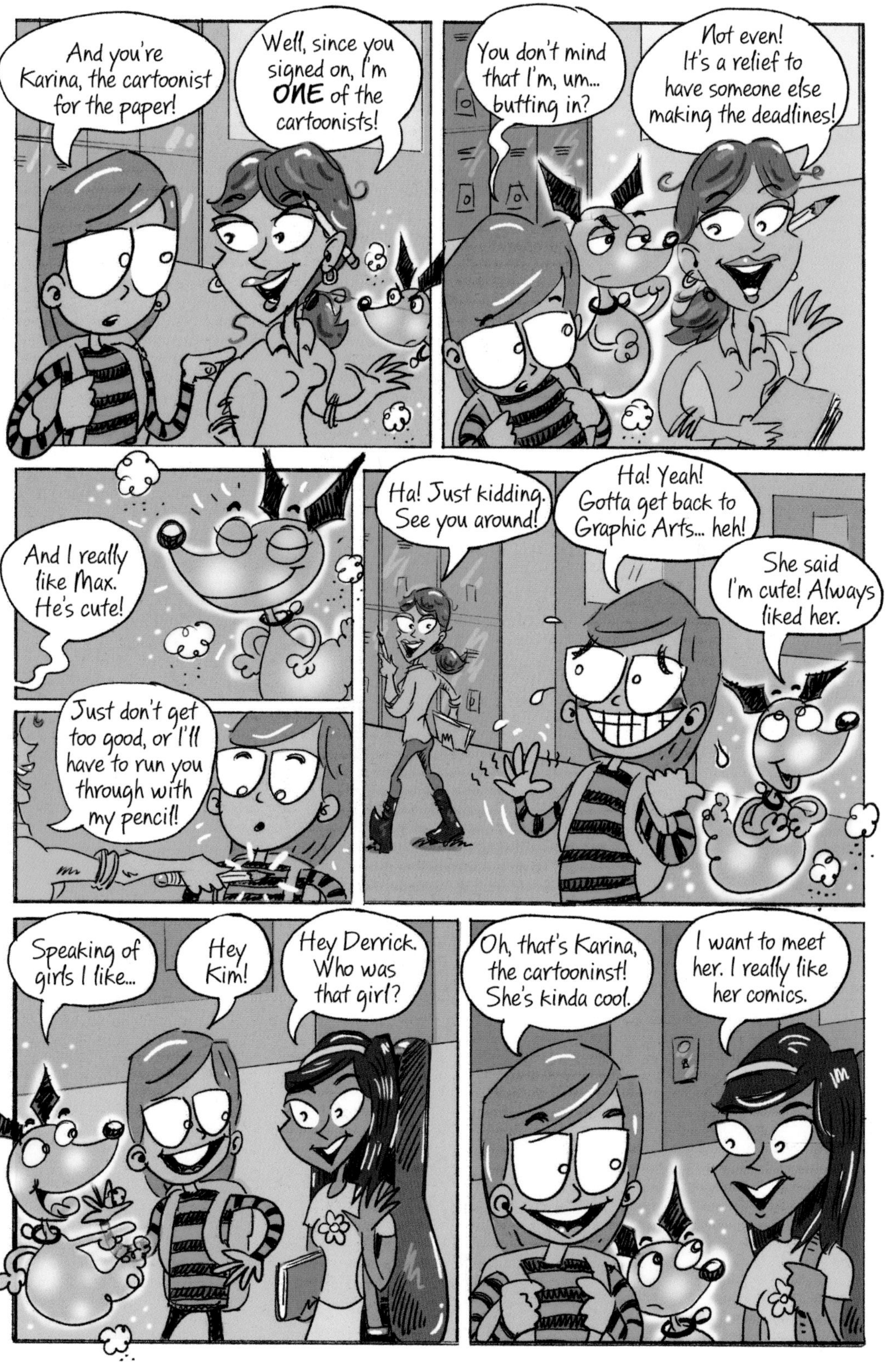
And you're Karina, the cartoonist for the paper!
Well, since you signed on, I'm **ONE** of the cartoonists!
You don't mind that I'm, um... butting in?
Not even! It's a relief to have someone else making the deadlines!
And I really like Max. He's cute!
Just don't get too good, or I'll have to run you through with my pencil!
Ha! Just kidding. See you around!
Ha! Yeah! Gotta get back to Graphic Arts... heh!
She said I'm cute! Always liked her.
Speaking of girls I like...
Hey Kim!
Hey Derrick. Who was that girl?
Oh, that's Karina, the cartooninst! She's kinda cool.
I want to meet her. I really like her comics.

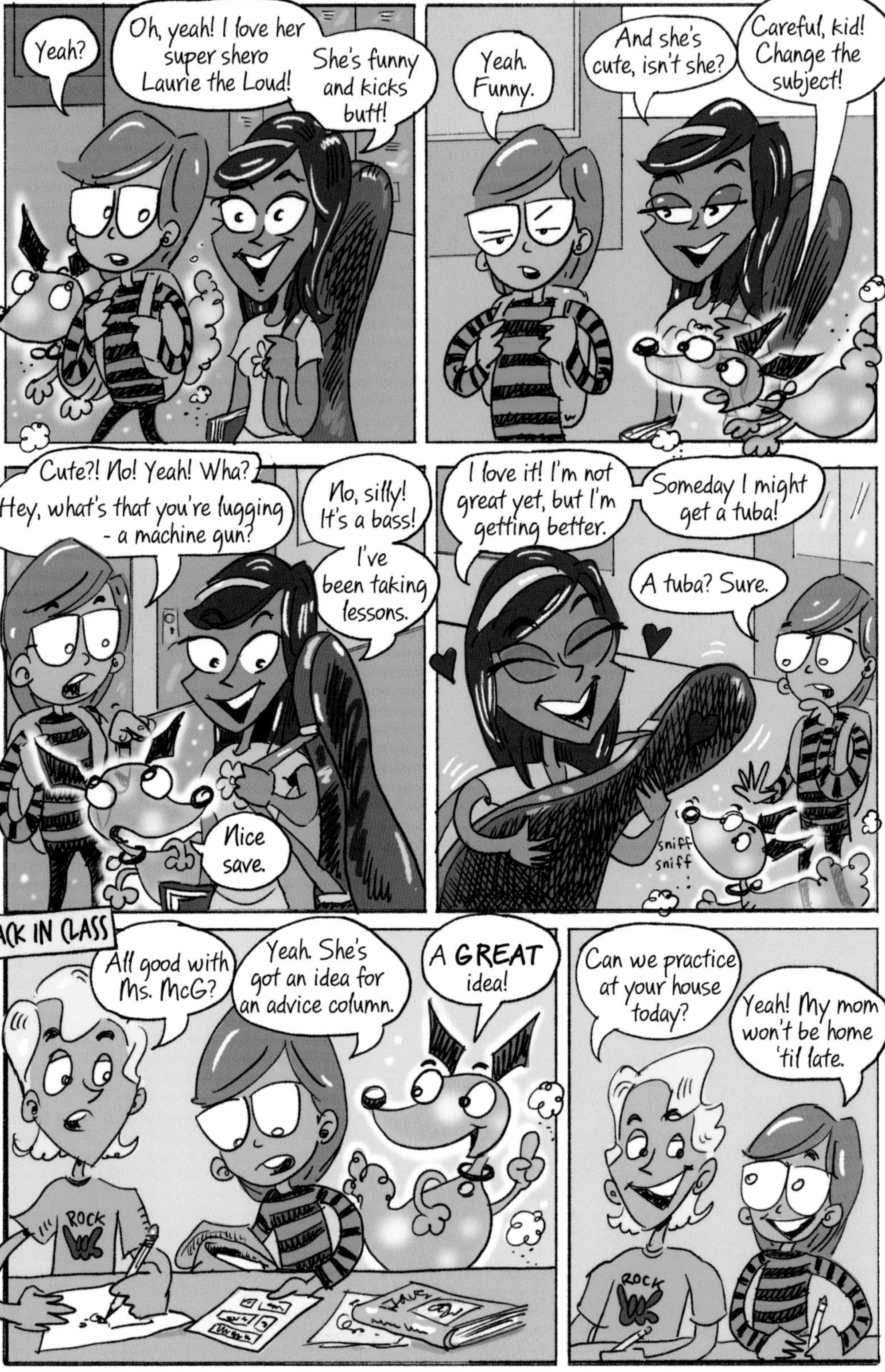
Yeah?
Oh, yeah! I love her super shero Laurie the Loud!
She's funny and kicks butt!
Yeah. Funny.
And she's cute, isn't she?
Careful, kid! Change the subject!
Cute?! No! Yeah! Wha? Hey, what's that you're lugging - a machine gun?
No, silly! It's a bass!
I've been taking lessons.
Nice save.
I love it! I'm not great yet, but I'm getting better.
Someday I might get a tuba!
A tuba? Sure.
sniff sniff
BACK IN CLASS
All good with Ms. McG?
Yeah. She's got an idea for an advice column.
A GREAT idea!
ROCK
Can we practice at your house today?
Yeah! My mom won't be home 'til late.
ROCK

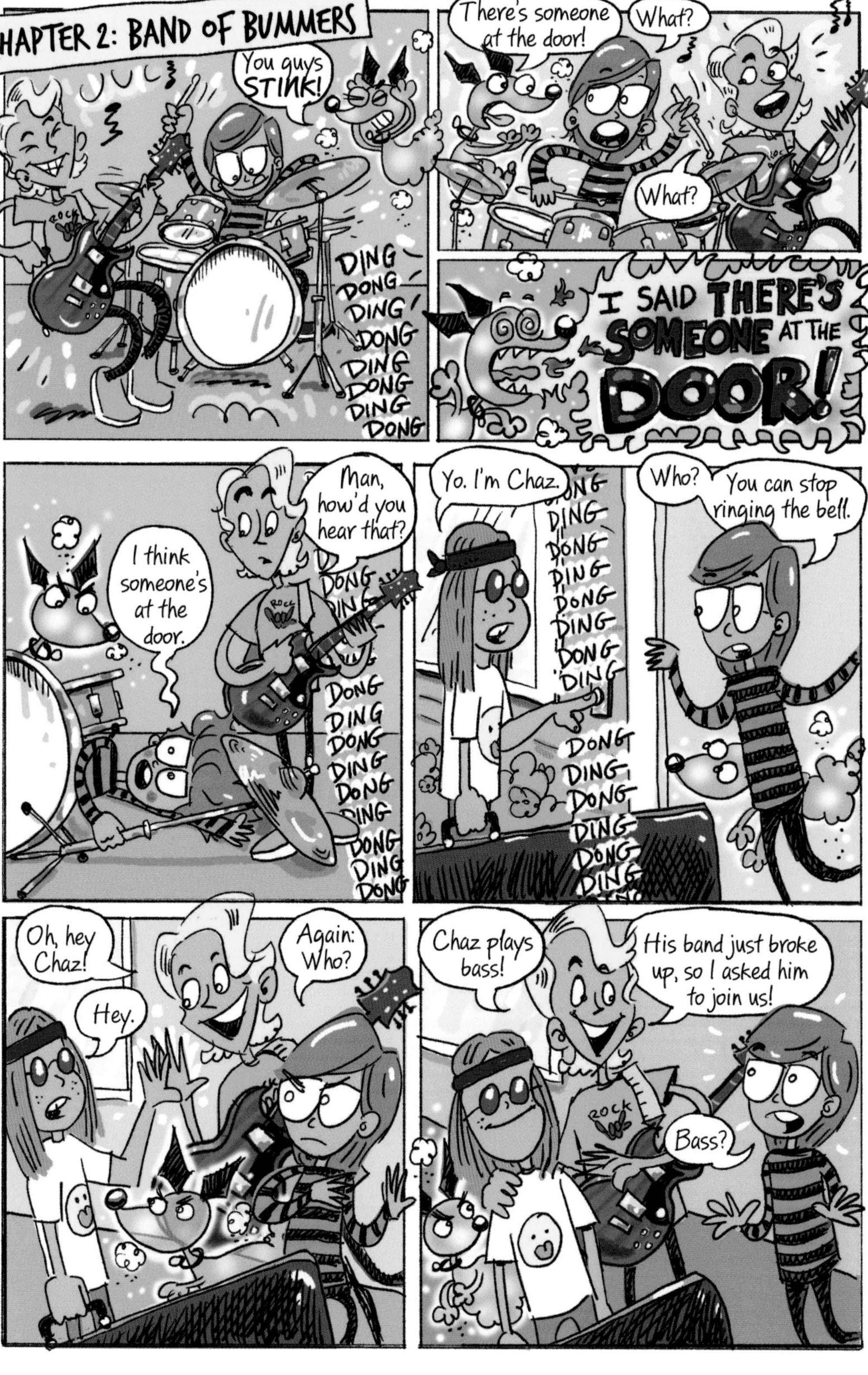
CHAPTER 2: BAND OF BUMMERS
You guys STINK!
DING DONG DING DONG DING DONG DING DONG
There's someone at the door!
What?
What?
I SAID THERE'S SOMEONE AT THE DOOR!
I think someone's at the door.
Man, how'd you hear that?
DONG DING DONG DING DONG DING DONG DING DONG
Yo. I'm Chaz.
DING DONG DING DONG DING DONG DING
Who?
You can stop ringing the bell.
DONG DING DONG DING DONG DING
Oh, hey Chaz!
Hey.
Again: Who?
Chaz plays bass!
His band just broke up, so I asked him to join us!
Bass?

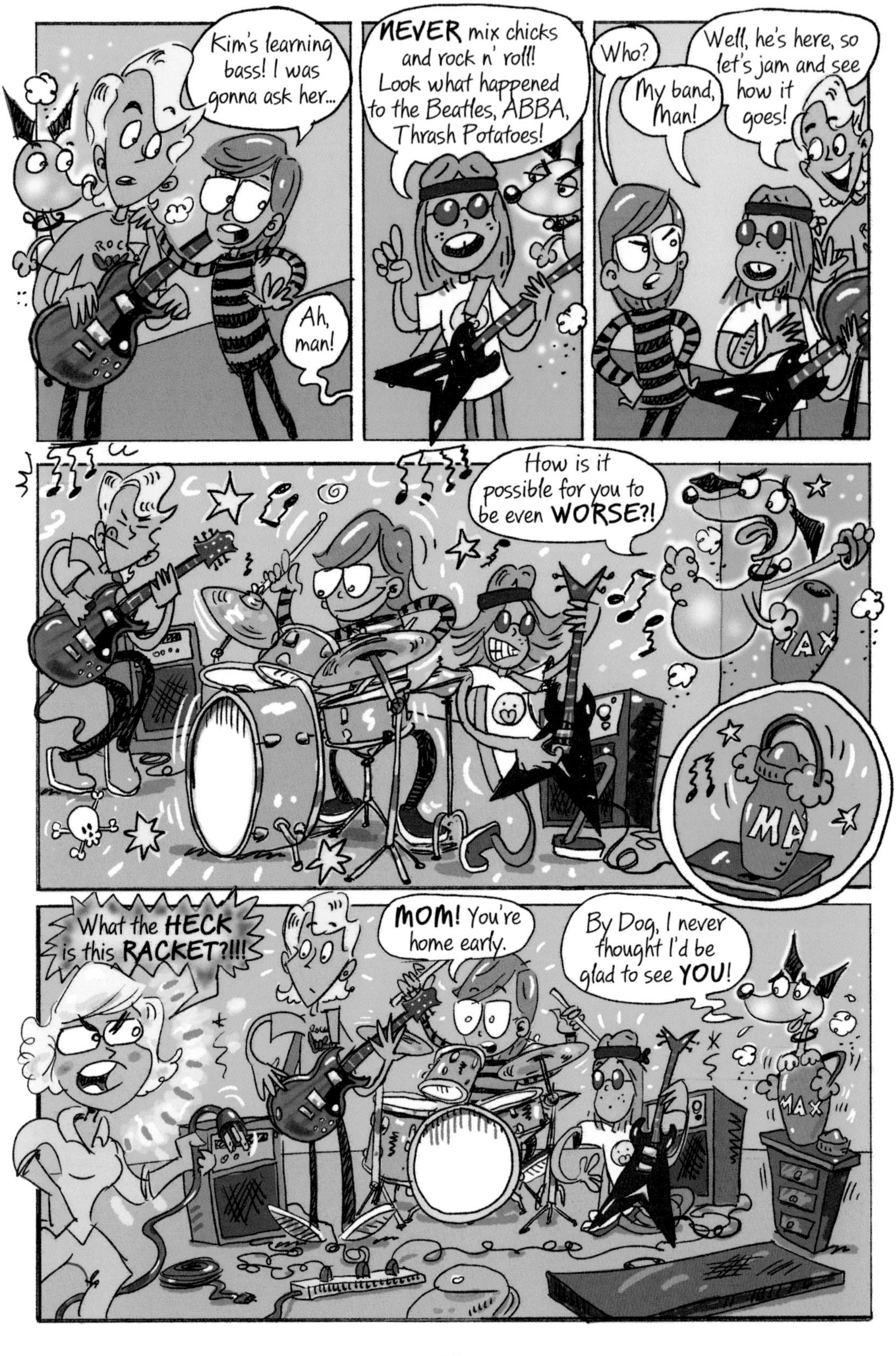
Kim's learning bass! I was gonna ask her...
Ah, man!
NEVER mix chicks and rock n' roll! Look what happened to the Beatles, ABBA, Thrash Potatoes!
Who?
My band, Man!
Well, he's here, so let's jam and see how it goes!
How is it possible for you to be even WORSE?!
MAX
MA
What the HECK is this RACKET?!!!
MOM! You're home early.
By Dog, I never thought I'd be glad to see YOU!
MAX

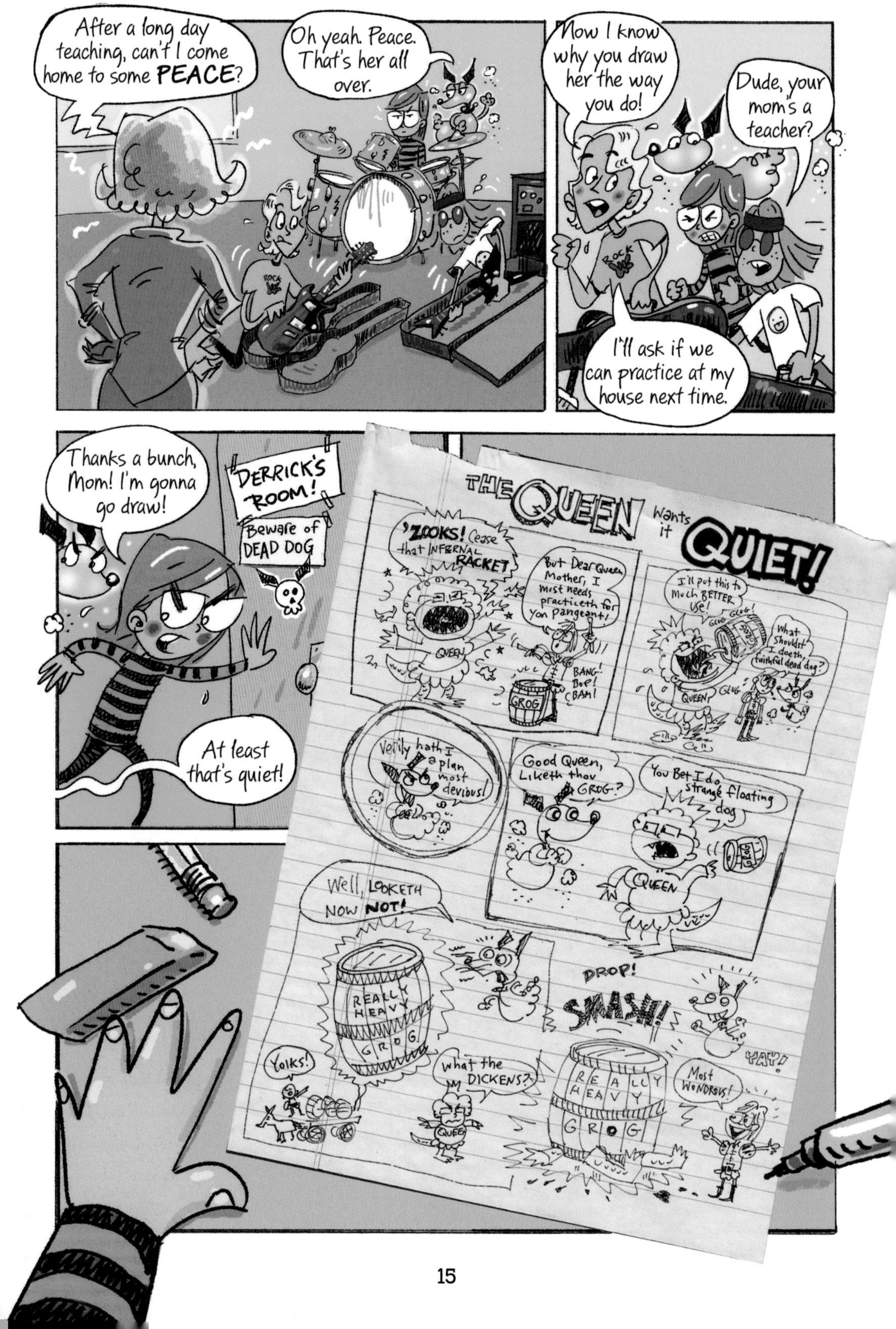

After a long day teaching, can't I come home to some PEACE?
Oh yeah. Peace. That's her all over.
Now I know why you draw her the way you do!
Dude, your mom's a teacher?
I'll ask if we can practice at my house next time.
Thanks a bunch, Mom! I'm gonna go draw!
DERRICK'S ROOM!
Beware of DEAD DOG
At least that's quiet!
THE QUEEN Wants it QUIET!
'ZOOKS! Cease that INFERNAL RACKET
But Dear Queen Mother, I must needs practiceth for yon pangeant!
QUEEN
BANG! BOP! BAM!
GROG
I'll put this to much BETTER use!
GLUG GLUG!
What shouldst I doeth, faithful dead dog?
QUEEN
GLUG
Verily hath I a plan most devious!
Good Queen, Liketh thou GROG?
You Bet I do strange floating dog
QUEEN
Well, LOOKETH NOW NOT!
REALLY HEAVY GROG
DROP!
SMASH!
YAY!
Yoiks!
What the DICKENS?
QUEEN
REALLY HEAVY GROG
Most Wondrous!

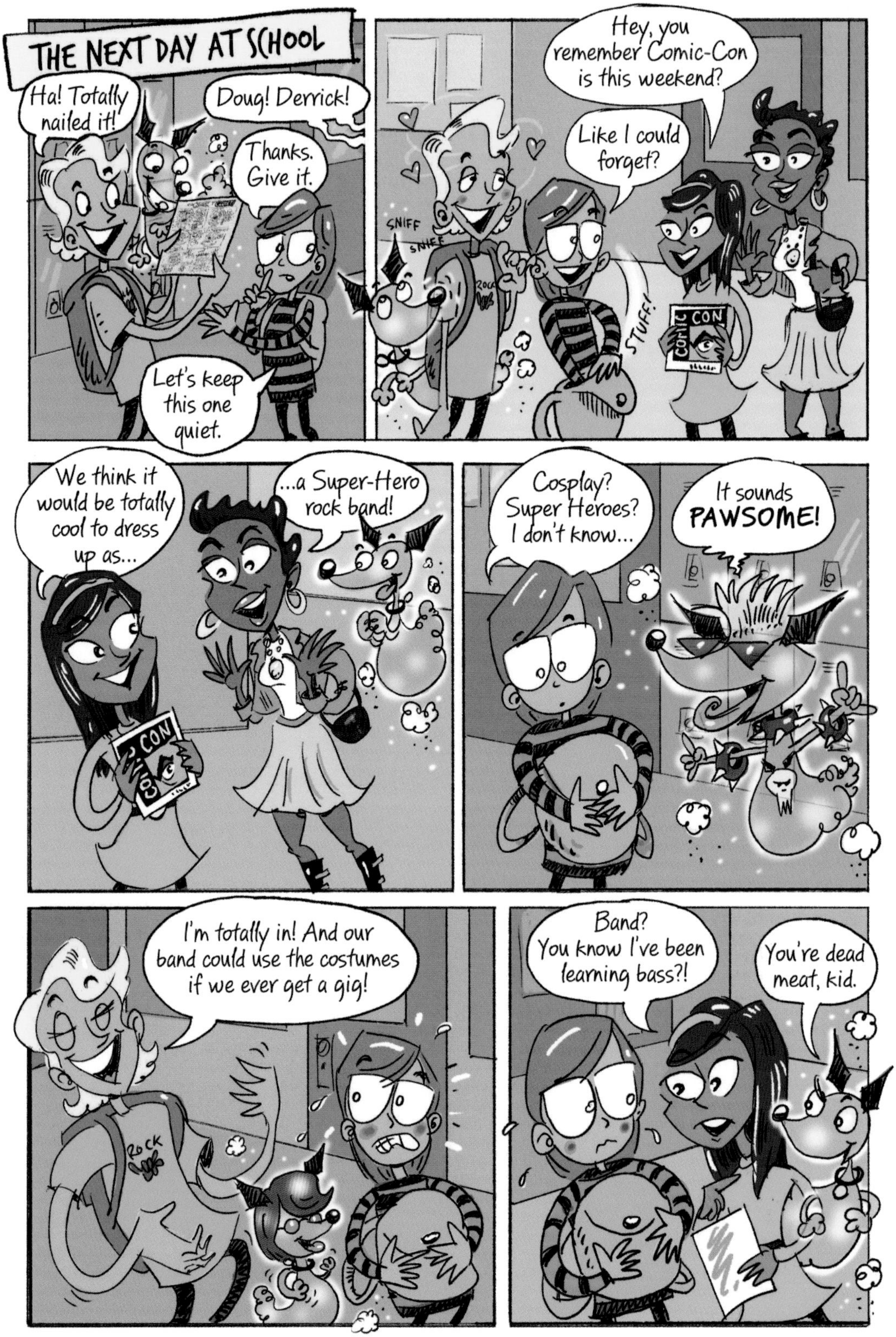
THE NEXT DAY AT SCHOOL
Ha! Totally nailed it!
Doug! Derrick!
Thanks. Give it.
Let's keep this one quiet.
Hey, you remember Comic-Con is this weekend?
Like I could forget?
SNIFF
SNIFF
STUFF!
COMIC CON
We think it would be totally cool to dress up as...
...a Super-Hero rock band!
Cosplay? Super Heroes? I don't know...
It sounds PAWSOME!
I'm totally in! And our band could use the costumes if we ever get a gig!
ROCK
Band? You know I've been learning bass?!
You're dead meat, kid.

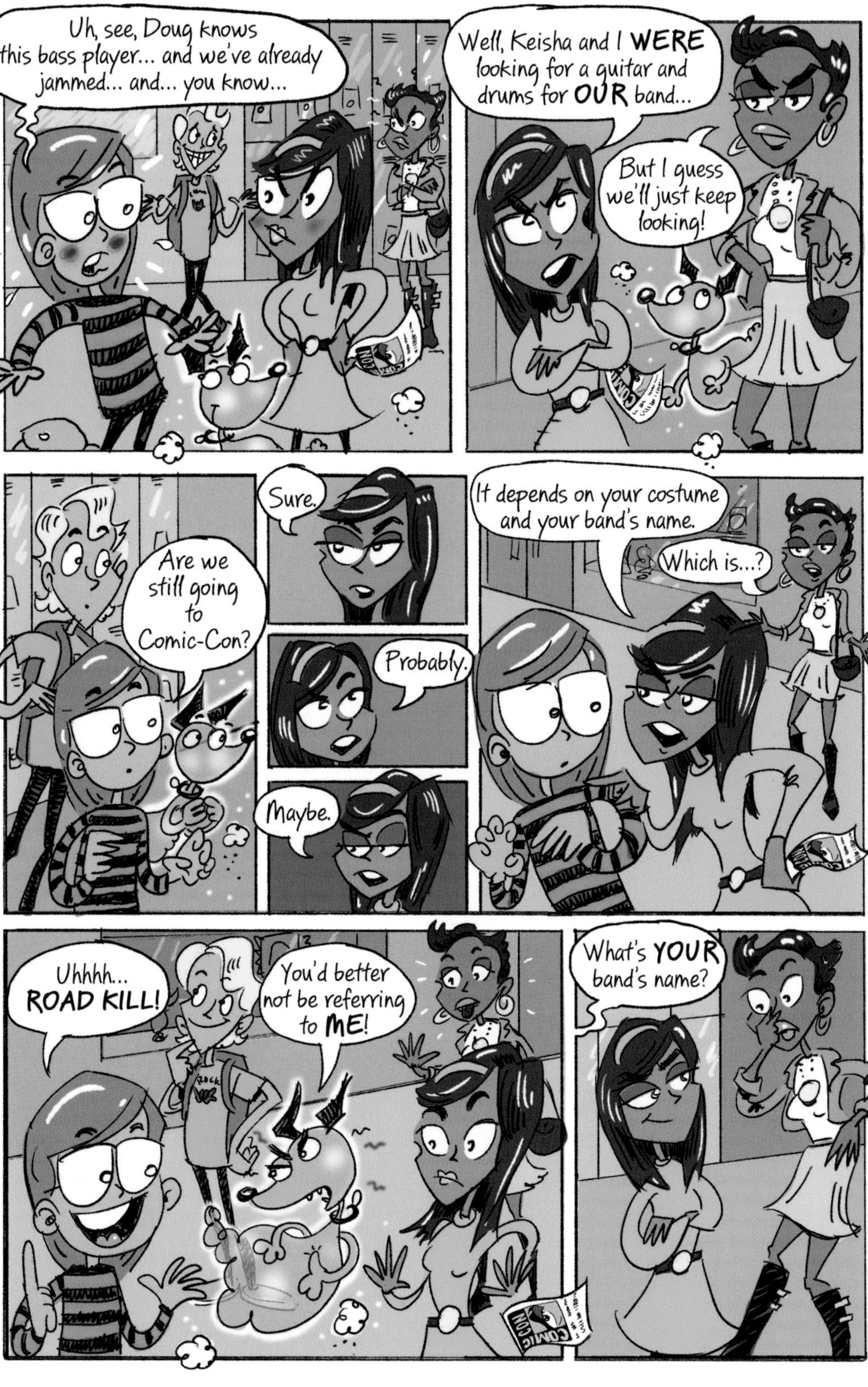

Uh, see, Doug knows this bass player... and we've already jammed... and... you know...
Well, Keisha and I WERE looking for a guitar and drums for OUR band...
But I guess we'll just keep looking!
Are we still going to Comic-Con?
Sure.
Probably.
Maybe.
It depends on your costume and your band's name.
Which is...?
Uhhhh... ROAD KILL!
You'd better not be referring to ME!
What's YOUR band's name?

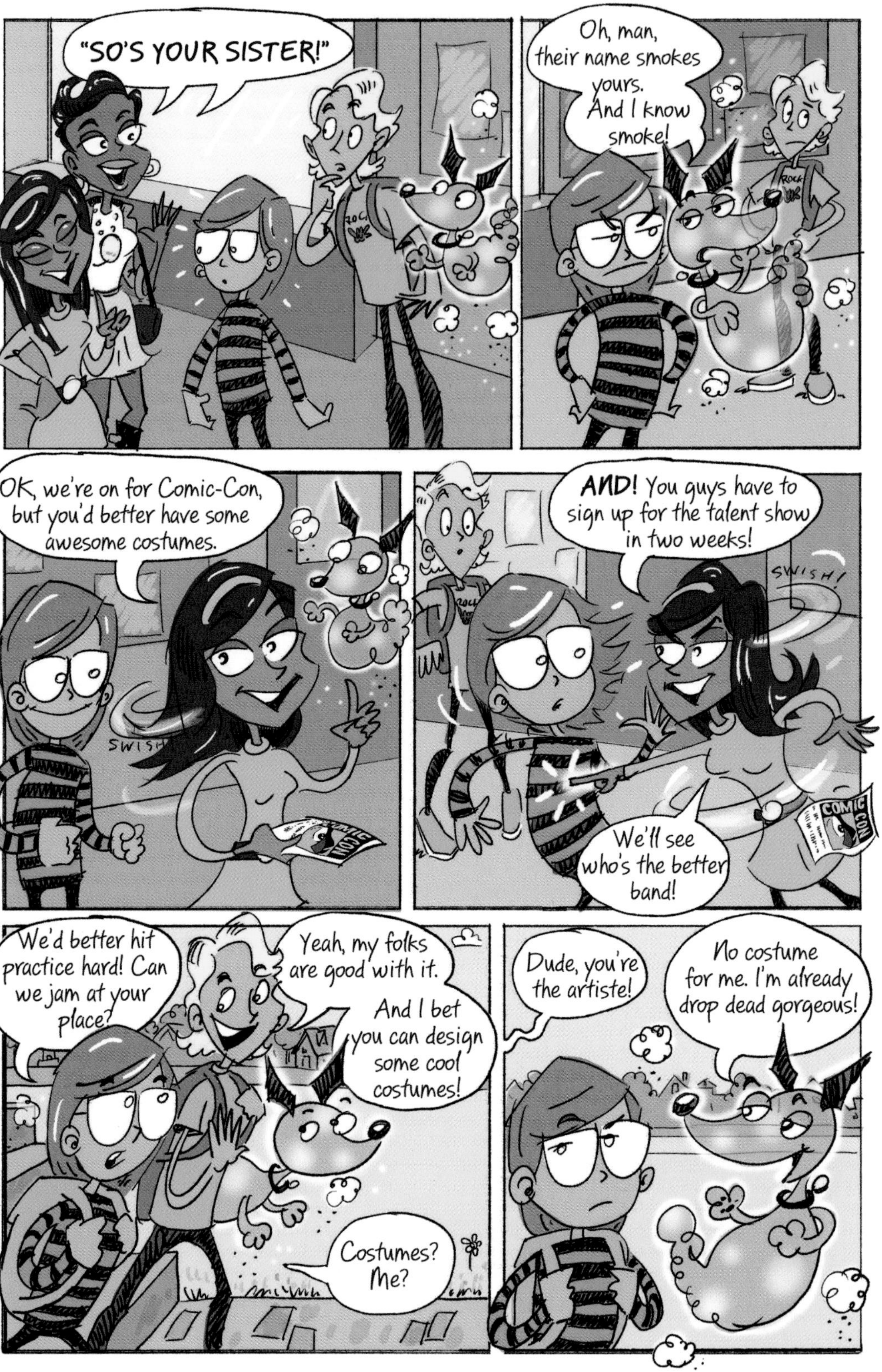
"SO'S YOUR SISTER!"
Oh, man, their name smokes yours. And I know smoke!
OK, we're on for Comic-Con, but you'd better have some awesome costumes.
SWISH
AND! You guys have to sign up for the talent show in two weeks!
SWISH!
We'll see who's the better band!
We'd better hit practice hard! Can we jam at your place?
Yeah, my folks are good with it.
And I bet you can design some cool costumes!
Costumes? Me?
Dude, you're the artiste!
No costume for me. I'm already drop dead gorgeous!

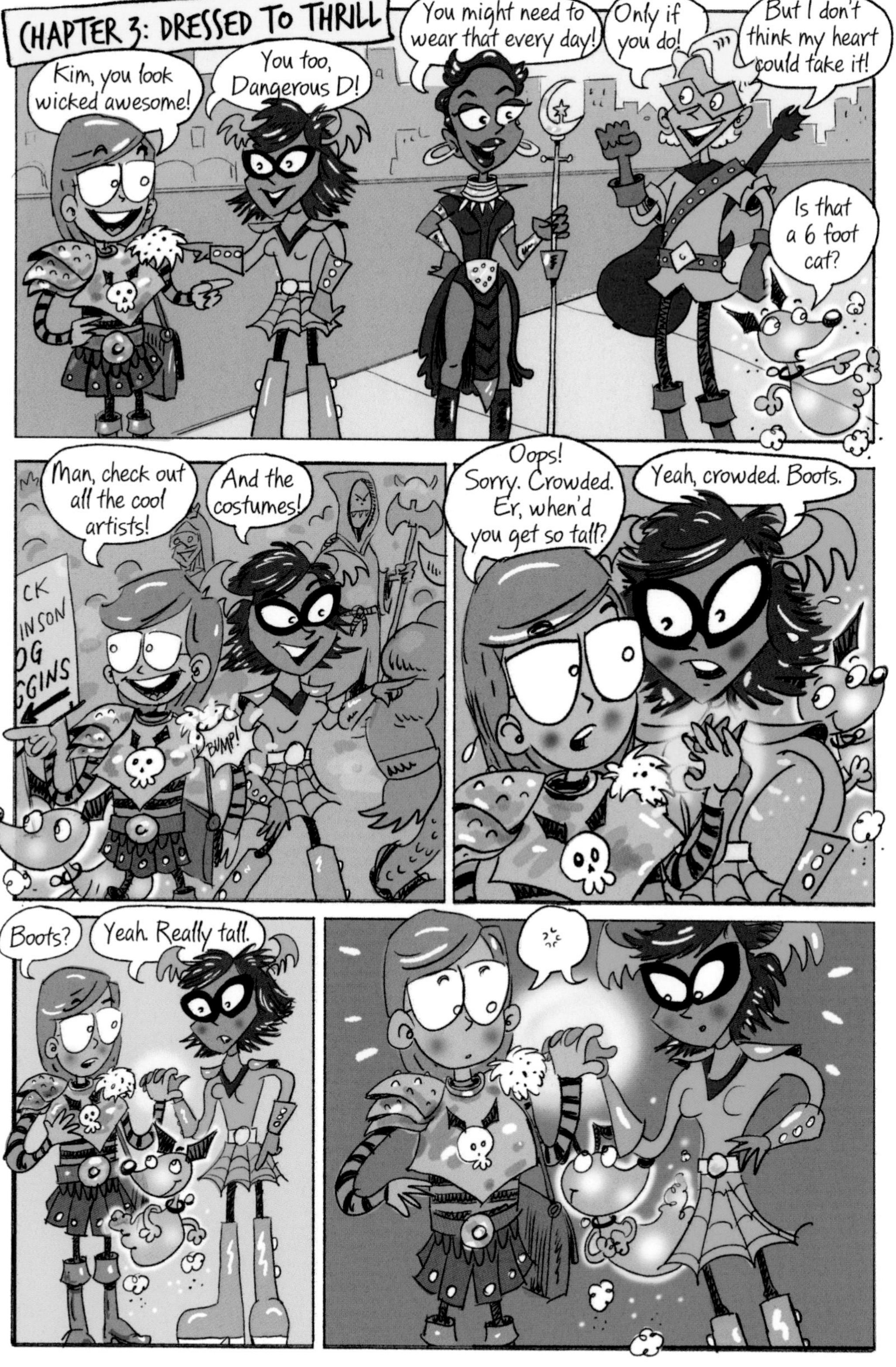
CHAPTER 3: DRESSED TO THRILL
Kim, you look wicked awesome!
You too, Dangerous D!
You might need to wear that every day!
Only if you do!
But I don't think my heart could take it!
Is that a 6 foot cat?
Man, check out all the cool artists!
And the costumes!
BUMP!
Oops! Sorry. Crowded. Er, when'd you get so tall?
Yeah, crowded. Boots.
Boots?
Yeah. Really tall.

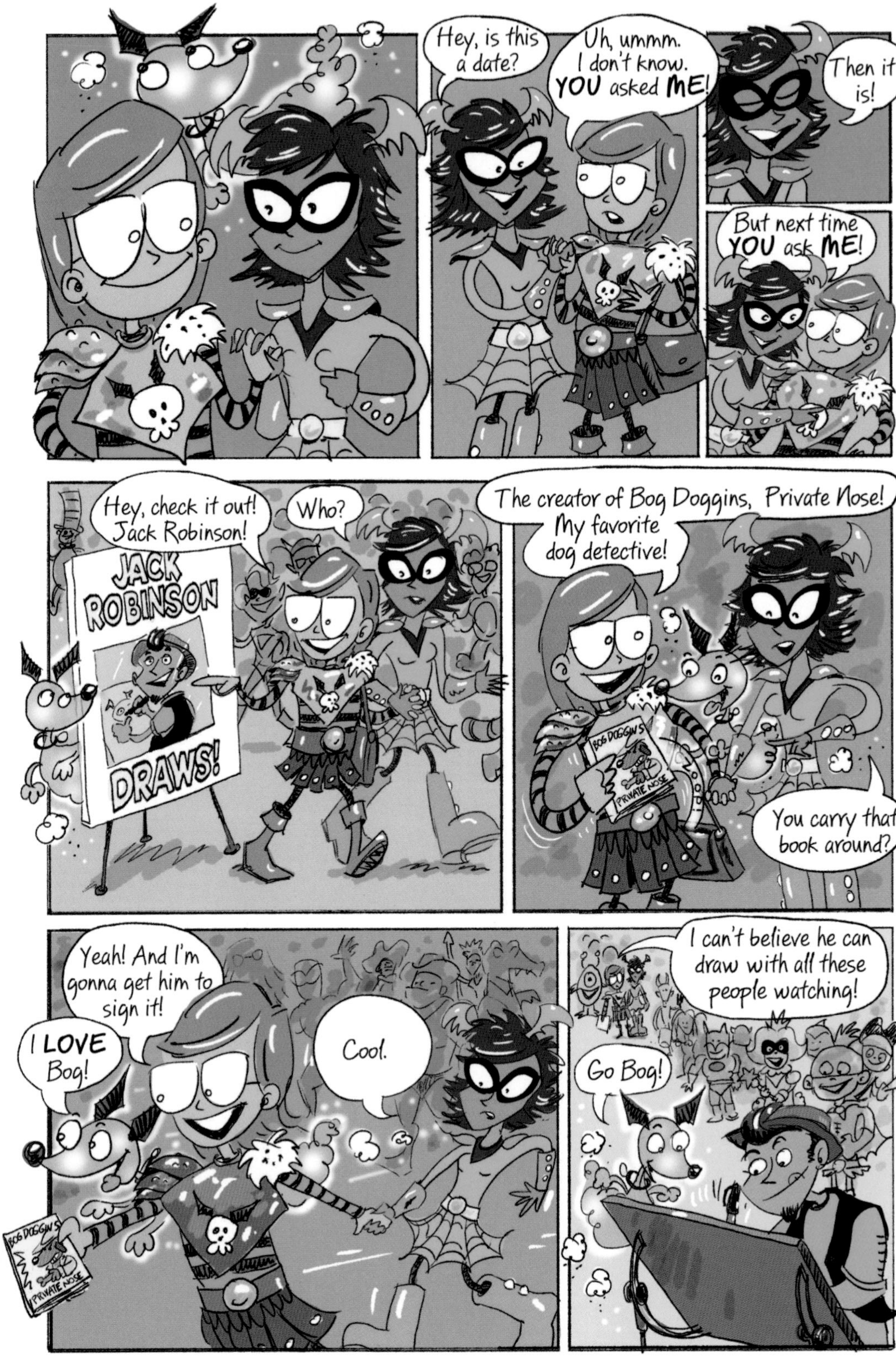
Hey, is this a date?
Uh, ummm. I don't know. YOU asked ME!
Then it is!
But next time YOU ask ME!
Hey, check it out! Jack Robinson!
JACK ROBINSON DRAWS!
Who?
The creator of Bog Doggins, Private Nose! My favorite dog detective!
BOG DOGGINS PRIVATE NOSE
You carry that book around?
Yeah! And I'm gonna get him to sign it!
I LOVE Bog!
Cool.
BOG DOGGINS PRIVATE NOSE
I can't believe he can draw with all these people watching!
Go Bog!

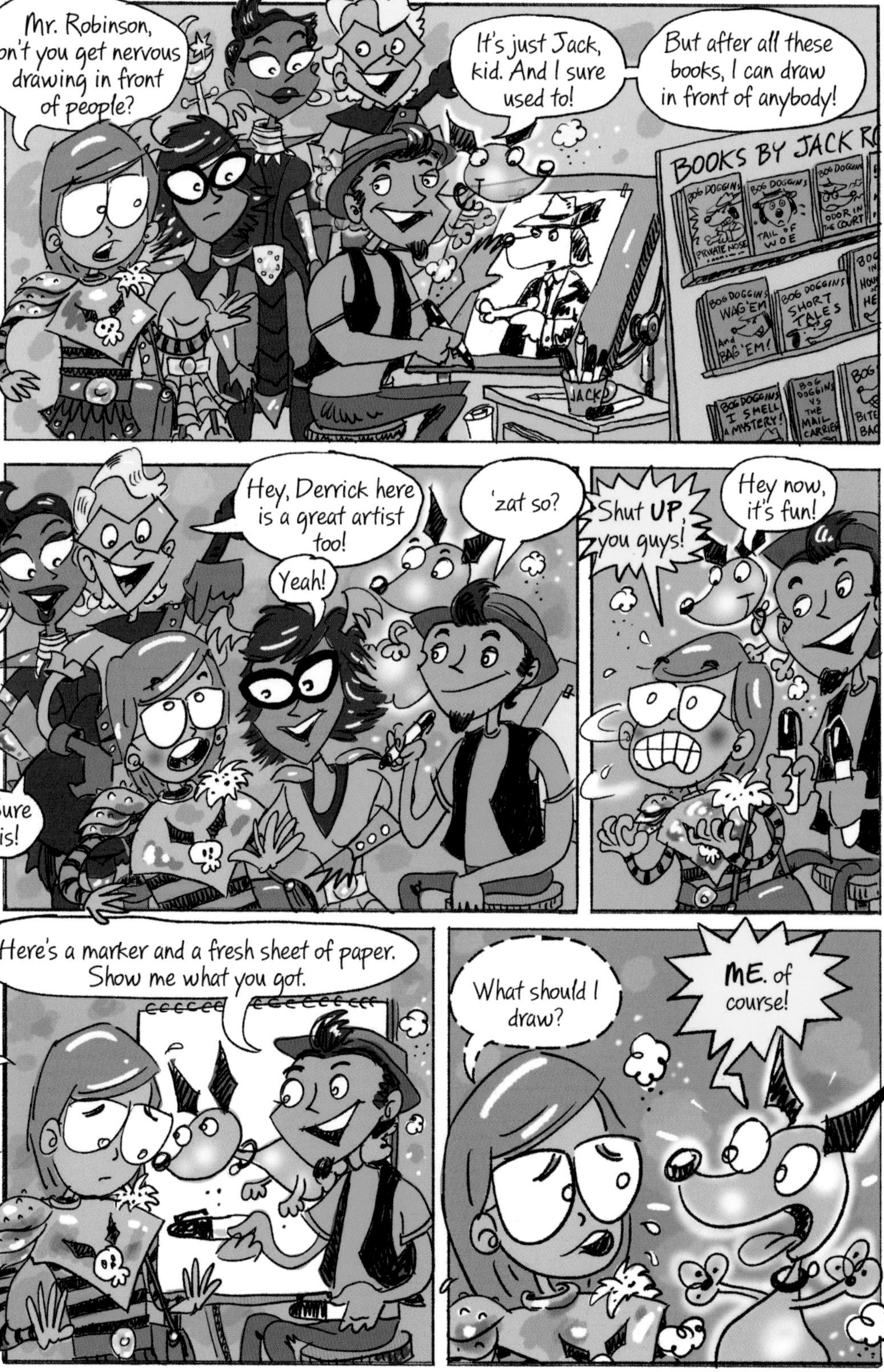
Mr. Robinson, don't you get nervous drawing in front of people?
It's just Jack, kid. And I sure used to!
But after all these books, I can draw in front of anybody!
BOOKS BY JACK RO
BOG DOGGINS PRIVATE NOSE
BOG DOGGINS TAIL OF WOE
BOG DOGGINS ODOR IN THE COURT
BOG DOGGINS WAG 'EM And BAG 'EM!
BOG DOGGINS SHORT TALES
BOG DOGGINS I SMELL A MYSTERY!
BOG DOGGINS VS THE MAIL CARRIER
JACK
Hey, Derrick here is a great artist too!
'zat so?
Yeah!
Sure is!
Shut UP, you guys!
Hey now, it's fun!
Here's a marker and a fresh sheet of paper. Show me what you got.
What should I draw?
ME. of course!

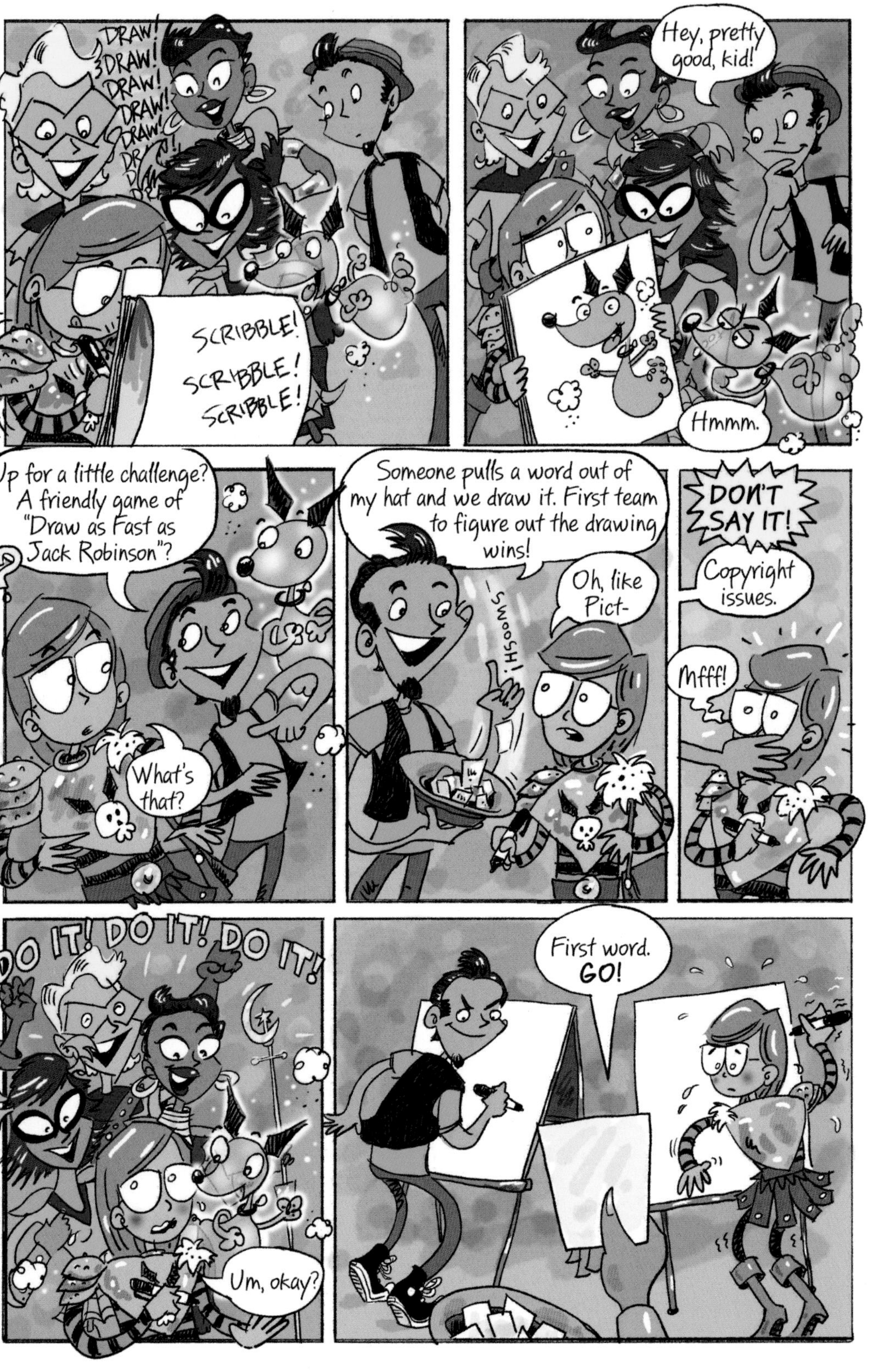
DRAW! DRAW! DRAW! DRAW! DRAW!
SCRIBBLE! SCRIBBLE! SCRIBBLE!
Hey, pretty good, kid!
Hmmm.
Up for a little challenge? A friendly game of "Draw as Fast as Jack Robinson"?
What's that?
Someone pulls a word out of my hat and we draw it. First team to figure out the drawing wins!
SWOOSH!
Oh, like Pict-
DON'T SAY IT!
Copyright issues.
Mfff!
DO IT! DO IT! DO IT!
Um, okay?
First word. GO!

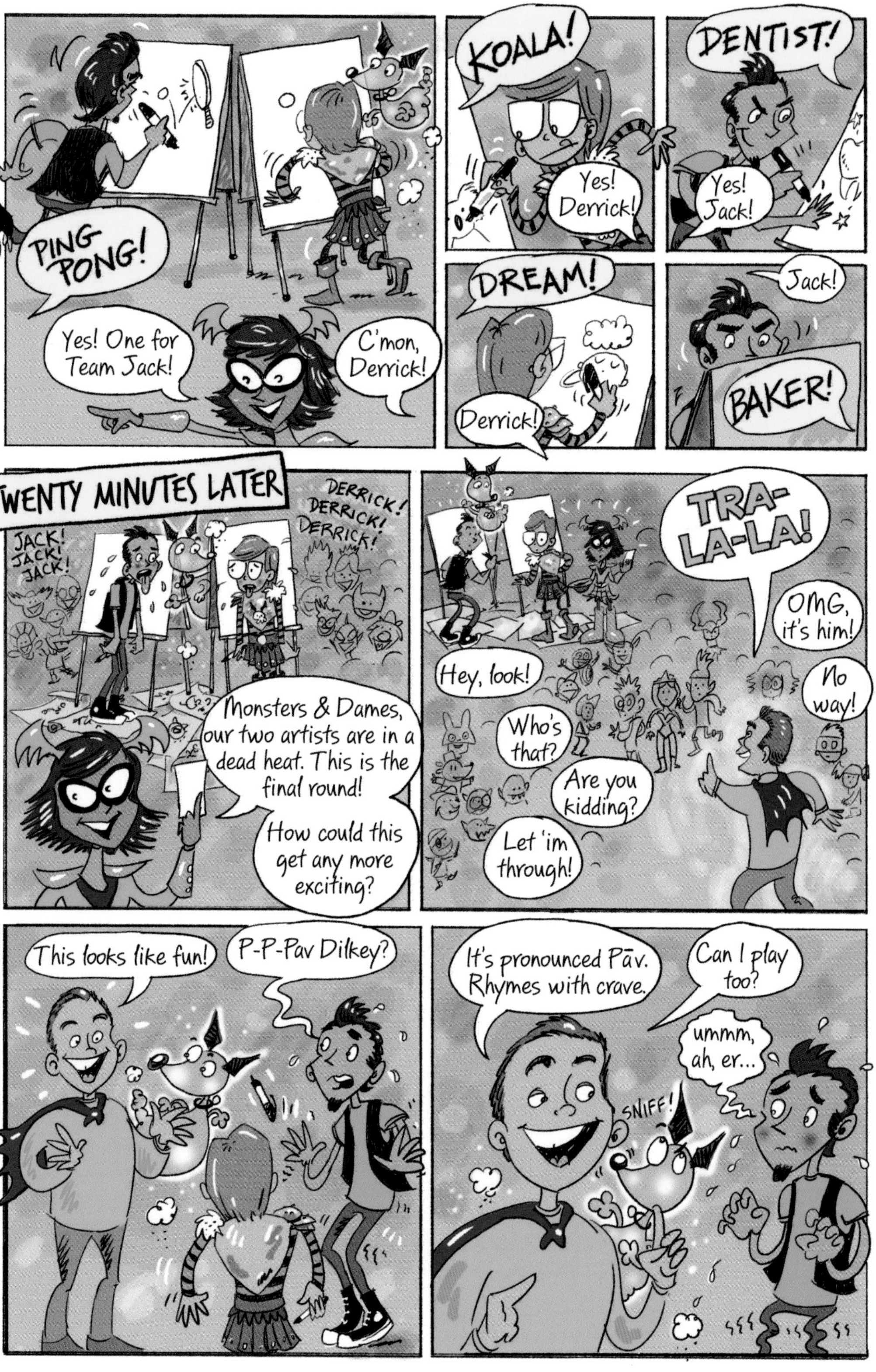
PING PONG!
Yes! One for Team Jack!
C'mon, Derrick!
KOALA!
Yes! Derrick!
DENTIST!
Yes! Jack!
DREAM!
Derrick!
Jack!
BAKER!
TWENTY MINUTES LATER
JACK! JACK! JACK!
DERRICK! DERRICK! DERRICK!
Monsters & Dames, our two artists are in a dead heat. This is the final round!
How could this get any more exciting?
TRA-LA-LA!
OMG, it's him!
Hey, look!
No way!
Who's that?
Are you kidding?
Let 'im through!
This looks like fun!
P-P-Pav Dilkey?
It's pronounced Pāv. Rhymes with crave.
Can I play too?
ummm, ah, er...
SNIFF!

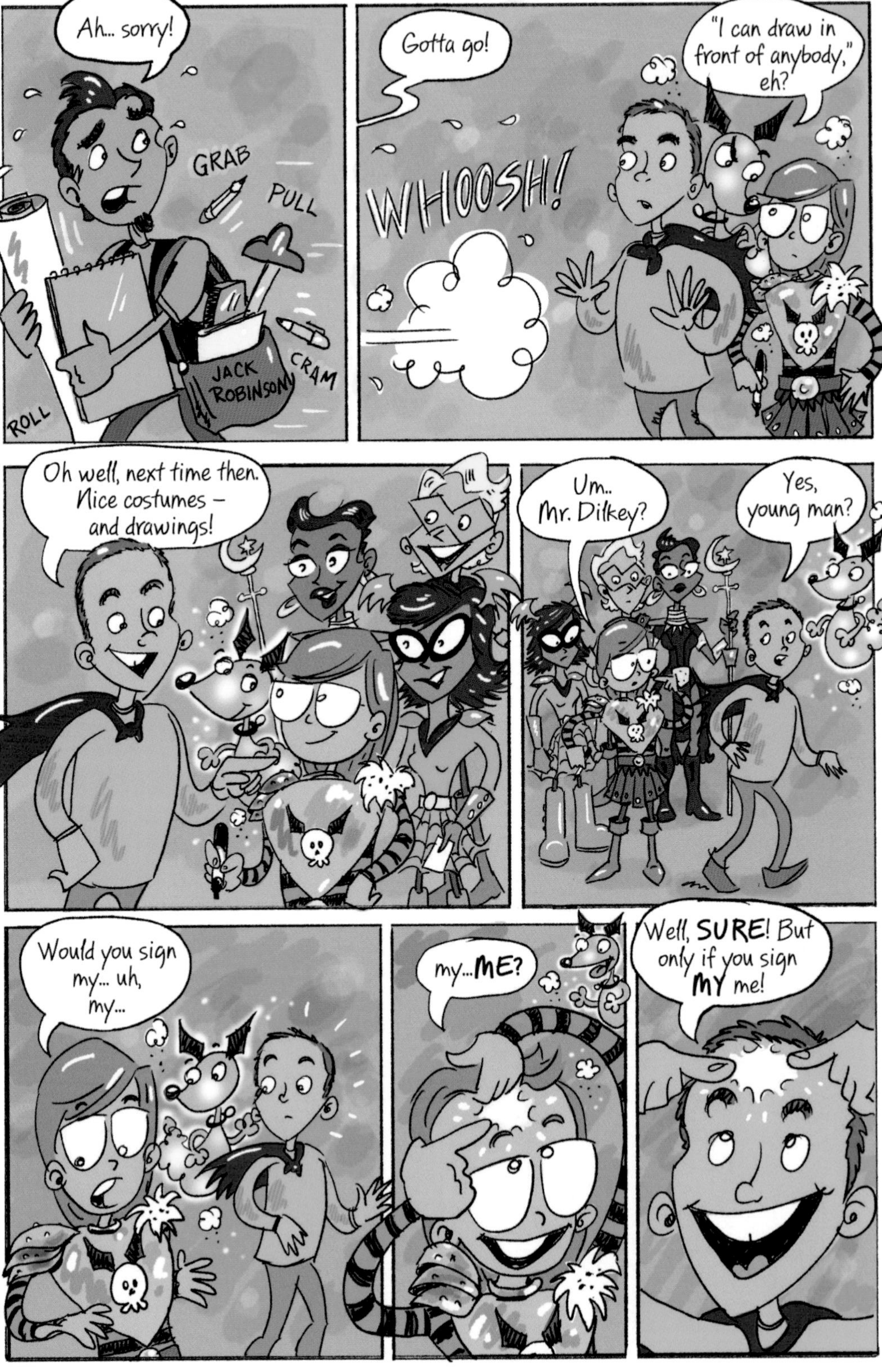
Ah... sorry!
GRAB
PULL
JACK ROBINSON
CRAM
ROLL
Gotta go!
WHOOSH!
"I can draw in front of anybody," eh?
Oh well, next time then. Nice costumes – and drawings!
Um.. Mr. Dilkey?
Yes, young man?
Would you sign my... uh, my...
my...ME?
Well, SURE! But only if you sign MY me!

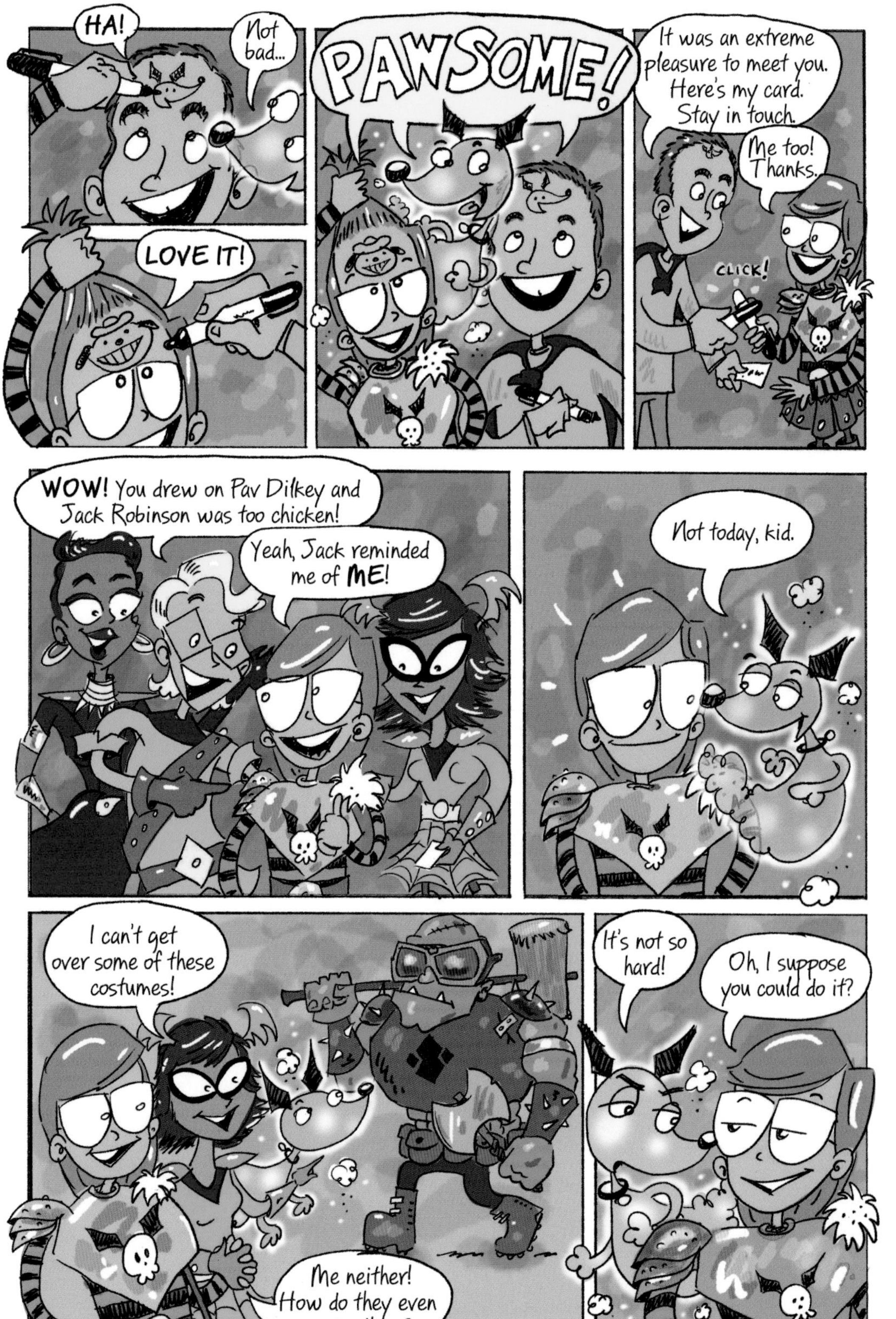
HA!
Not bad...
LOVE IT!
PAWSOME!
It was an extreme pleasure to meet you. Here's my card. Stay in touch.
Me too! Thanks.
CLICK!
WOW! You drew on Pav Dilkey and Jack Robinson was too chicken!
Yeah, Jack reminded me of ME!
Not today, kid.
I can't get over some of these costumes!
Me neither! How do they even make them?
It's not so hard!
Oh, I suppose you could do it?

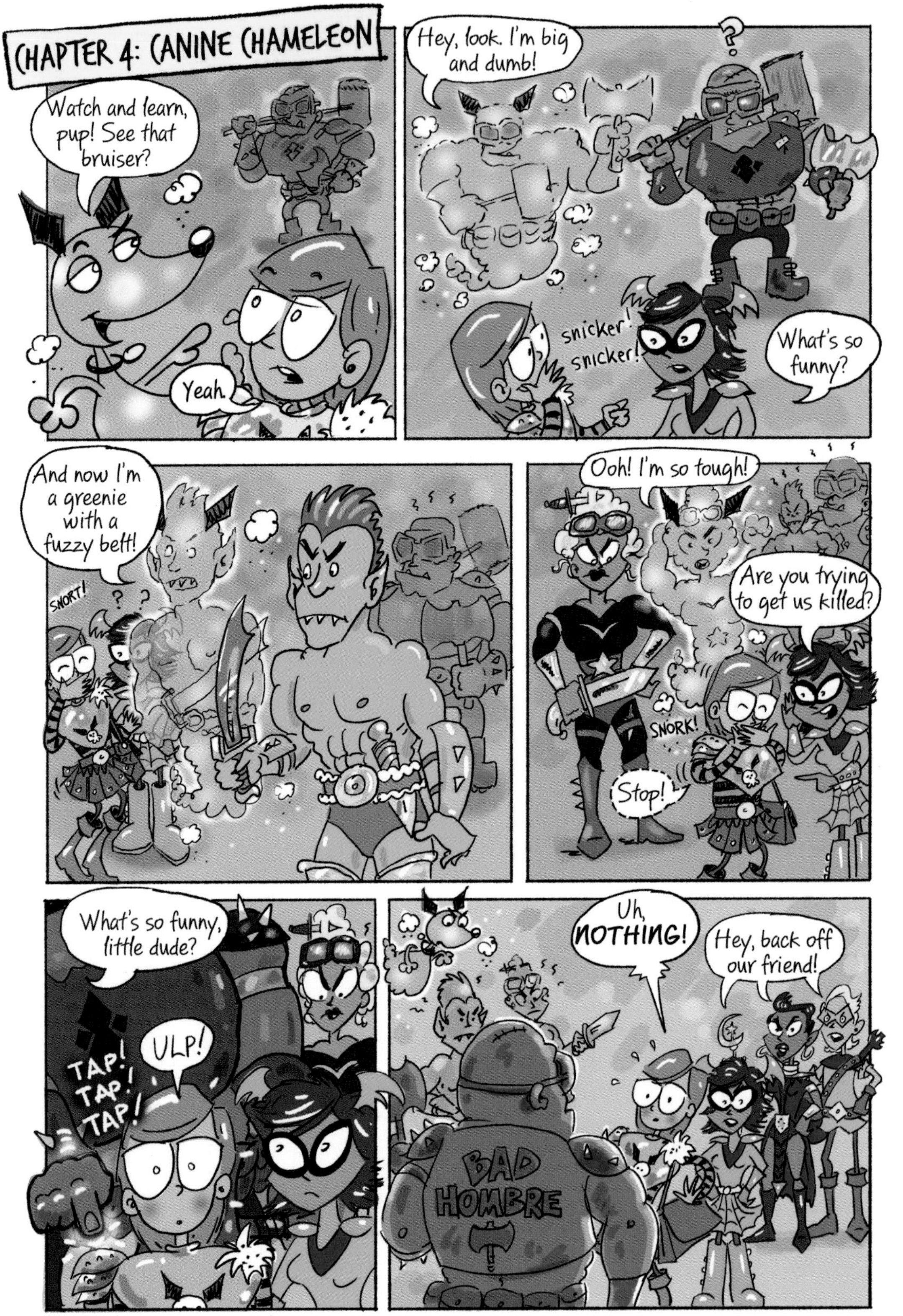
CHAPTER 4: CANINE CHAMELEON
Watch and learn, pup! See that bruiser?
Yeah.
Hey, look. I'm big and dumb!
?
snicker! snicker!
What's so funny?
And now I'm a greenie with a fuzzy belt!
SNORT!
? ?
Ooh! I'm so tough!
Are you trying to get us killed?
SNORK!
Stop!
What's so funny, little dude?
ULP!
TAP! TAP! TAP!
Uh, NOTHING!
Hey, back off our friend!
BAD HOMBRE

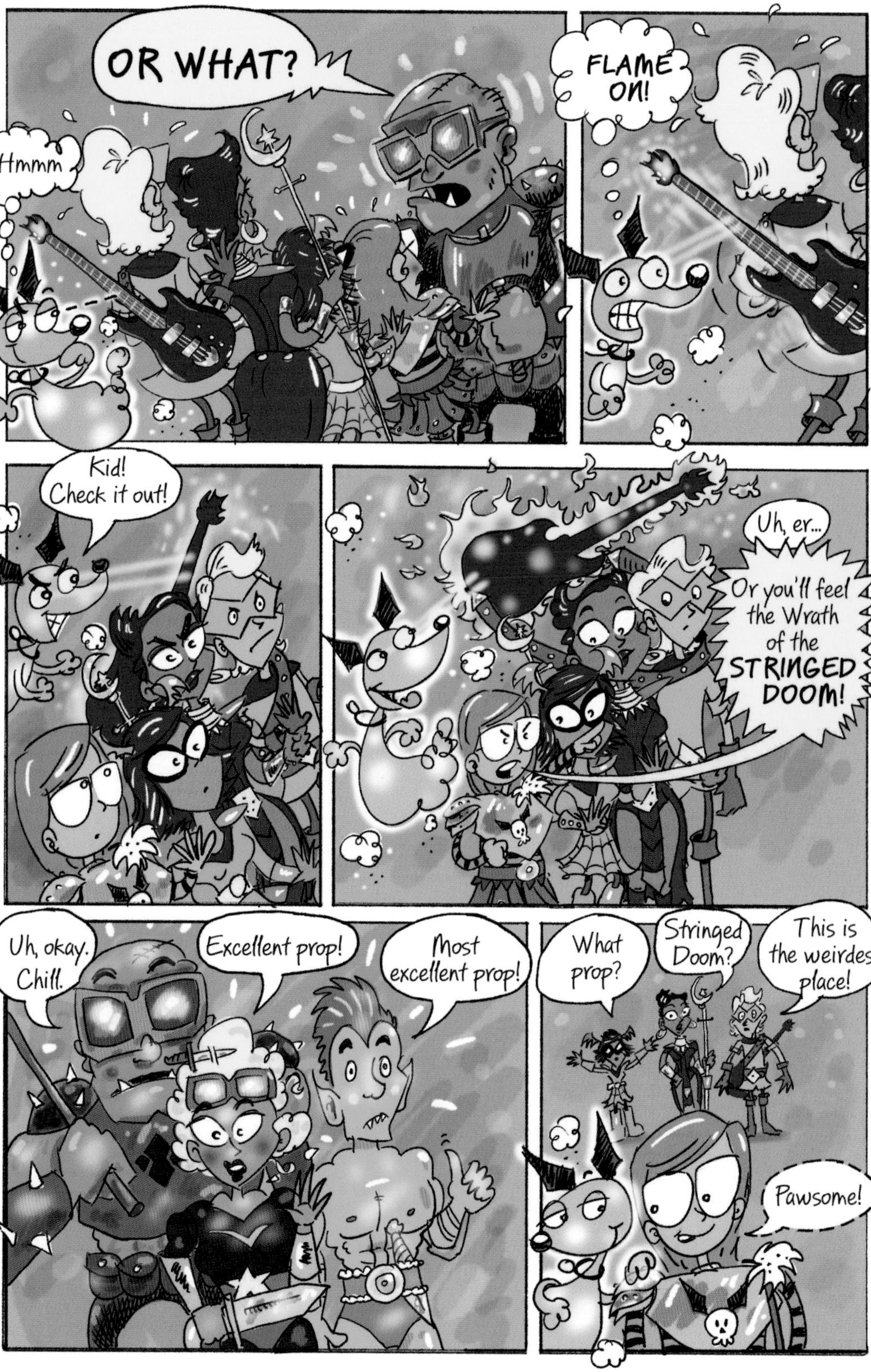
OR WHAT?
Hmmm
FLAME ON!
Kid! Check it out!
Uh, er...
Or you'll feel the Wrath of the STRINGED DOOM!
Uh, okay. Chill.
Excellent prop!
Most excellent prop!
What prop?
Stringed Doom?
This is the weirdest place!
Pawsome!

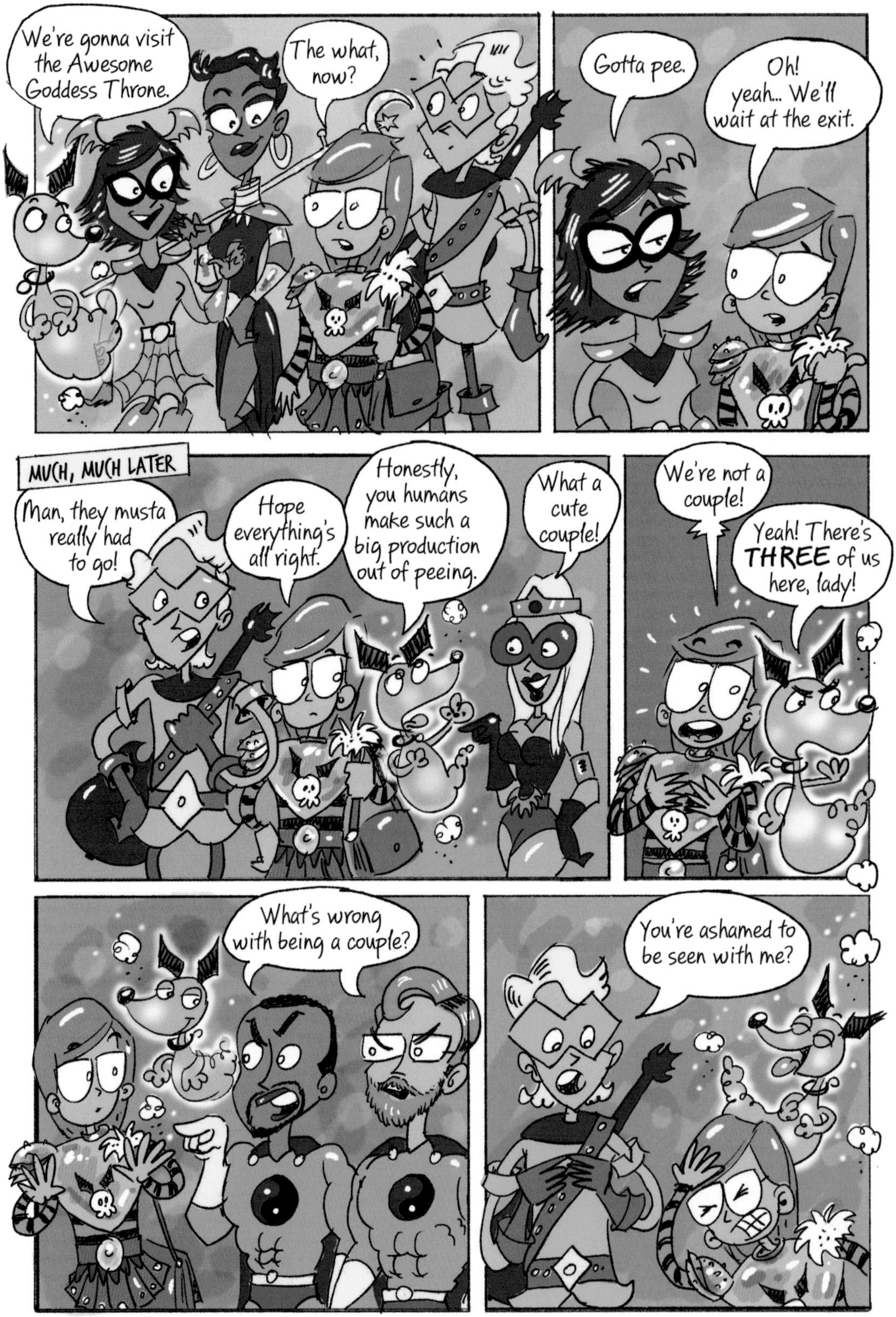
We're gonna visit the Awesome Goddess Throne.
The what, now?
Gotta pee.
Oh! yeah... We'll wait at the exit.
MUCH, MUCH LATER
Man, they musta really had to go!
Hope everything's all right.
Honestly, you humans make such a big production out of peeing.
What a cute couple!
We're not a couple!
Yeah! There's THREE of us here, lady!
What's wrong with being a couple?
You're ashamed to be seen with me?

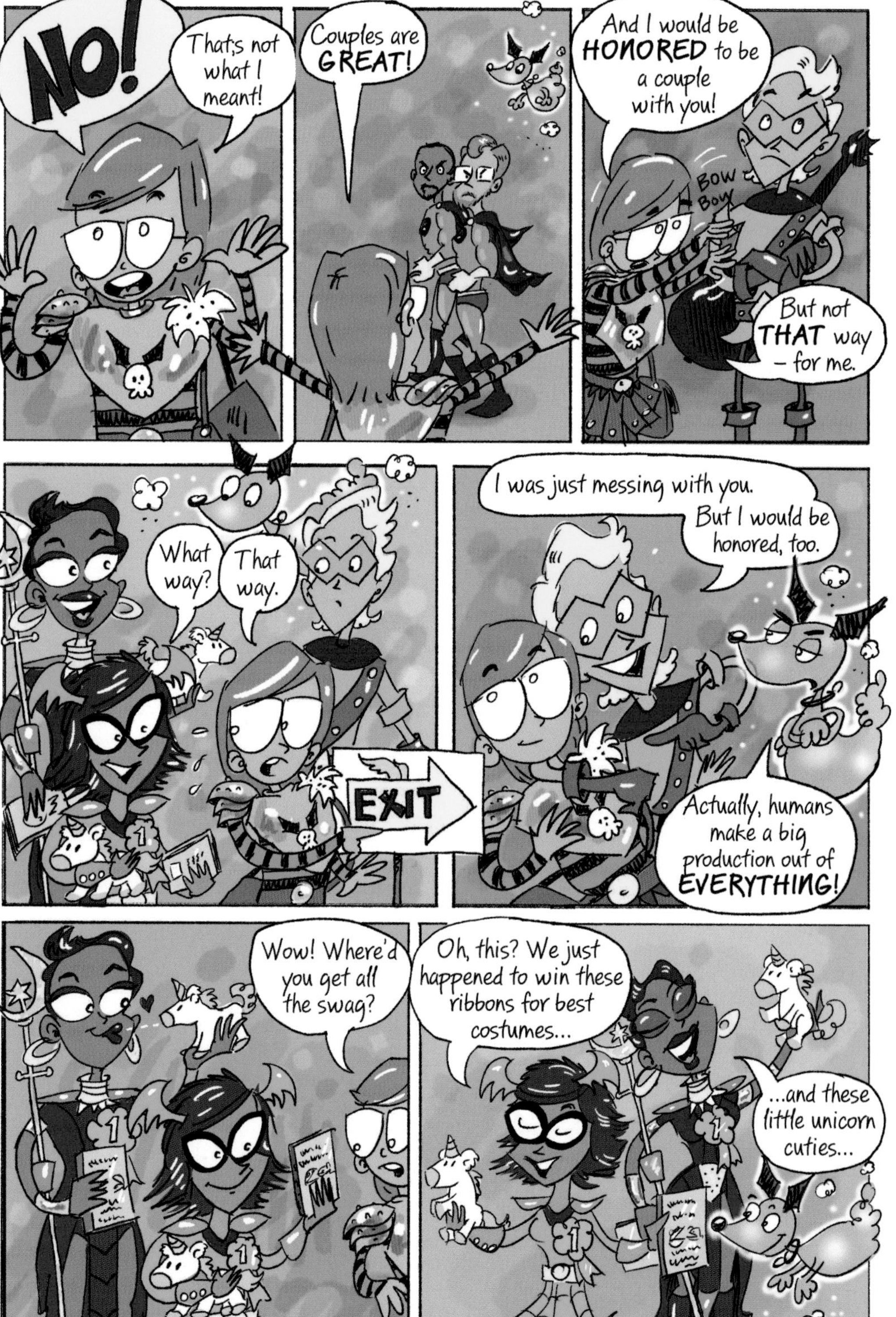
NO!
That;s not what I meant!
Couples are GREAT!
And I would be HONORED to be a couple with you!
BOW BOW
But not THAT way – for me.
What way?
That way.
EXIT
I was just messing with you.
But I would be honored, too.
Actually, humans make a big production out of EVERYTHING!
Wow! Where'd you get all the swag?
Oh, this? We just happened to win these ribbons for best costumes...
...and these little unicorn cuties...

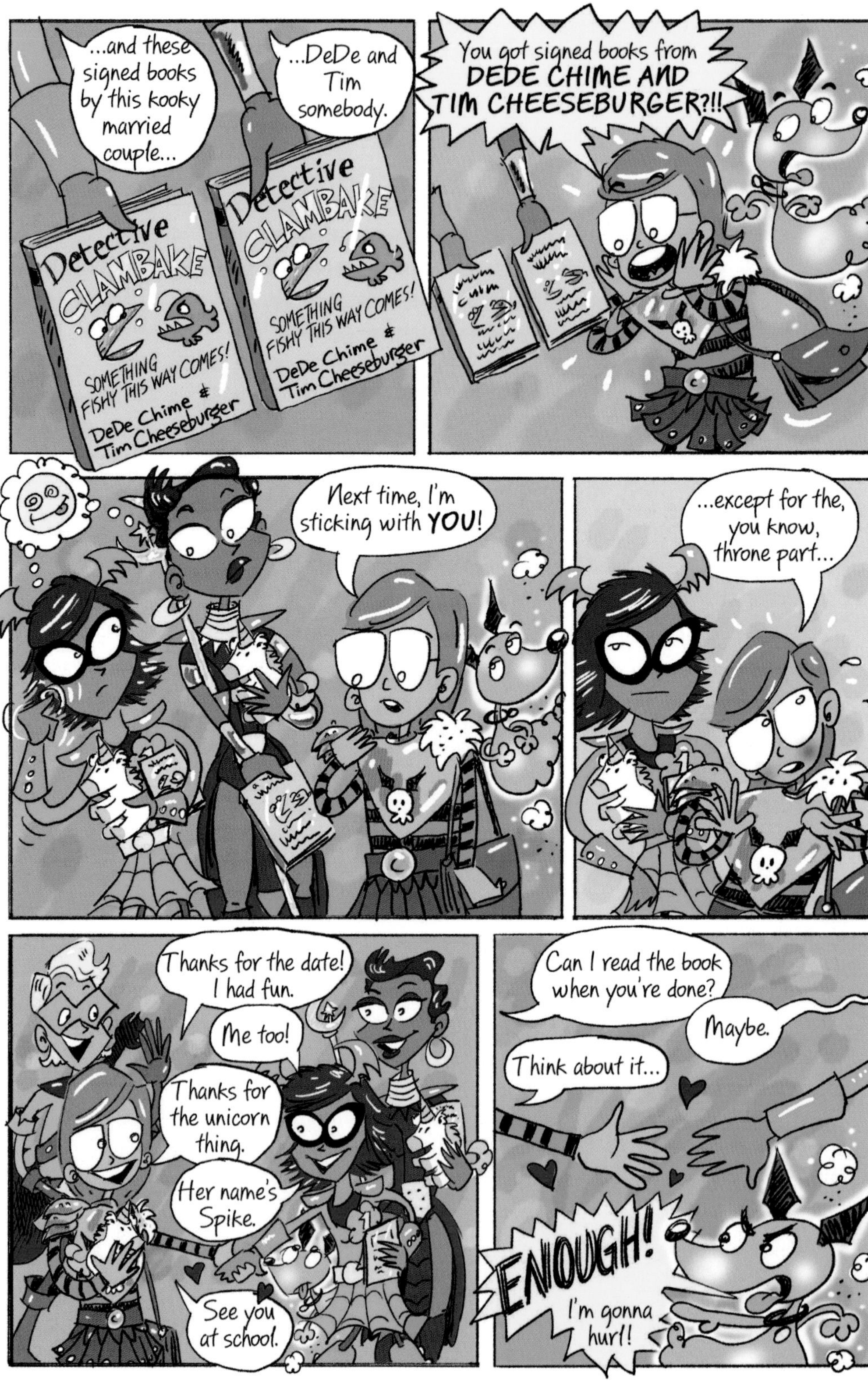
...and these signed books by this kooky married couple...
...DeDe and Tim somebody.
Detective CLAMBAKE
SOMETHING FISHY THIS WAY COMES!
DeDe Chime & Tim Cheeseburger
Detective CLAMBAKE
SOMETHING FISHY THIS WAY COMES!
DeDe Chime & Tim Cheeseburger
You got signed books from DEDE CHIME AND TIM CHEESEBURGER?!!
Next time, I'm sticking with YOU!
...except for the, you know, throne part...
Thanks for the date! I had fun.
Me too!
Thanks for the unicorn thing.
Her name's Spike.
See you at school.
Can I read the book when you're done?
Maybe.
Think about it...
ENOUGH!
I'm gonna hurl!

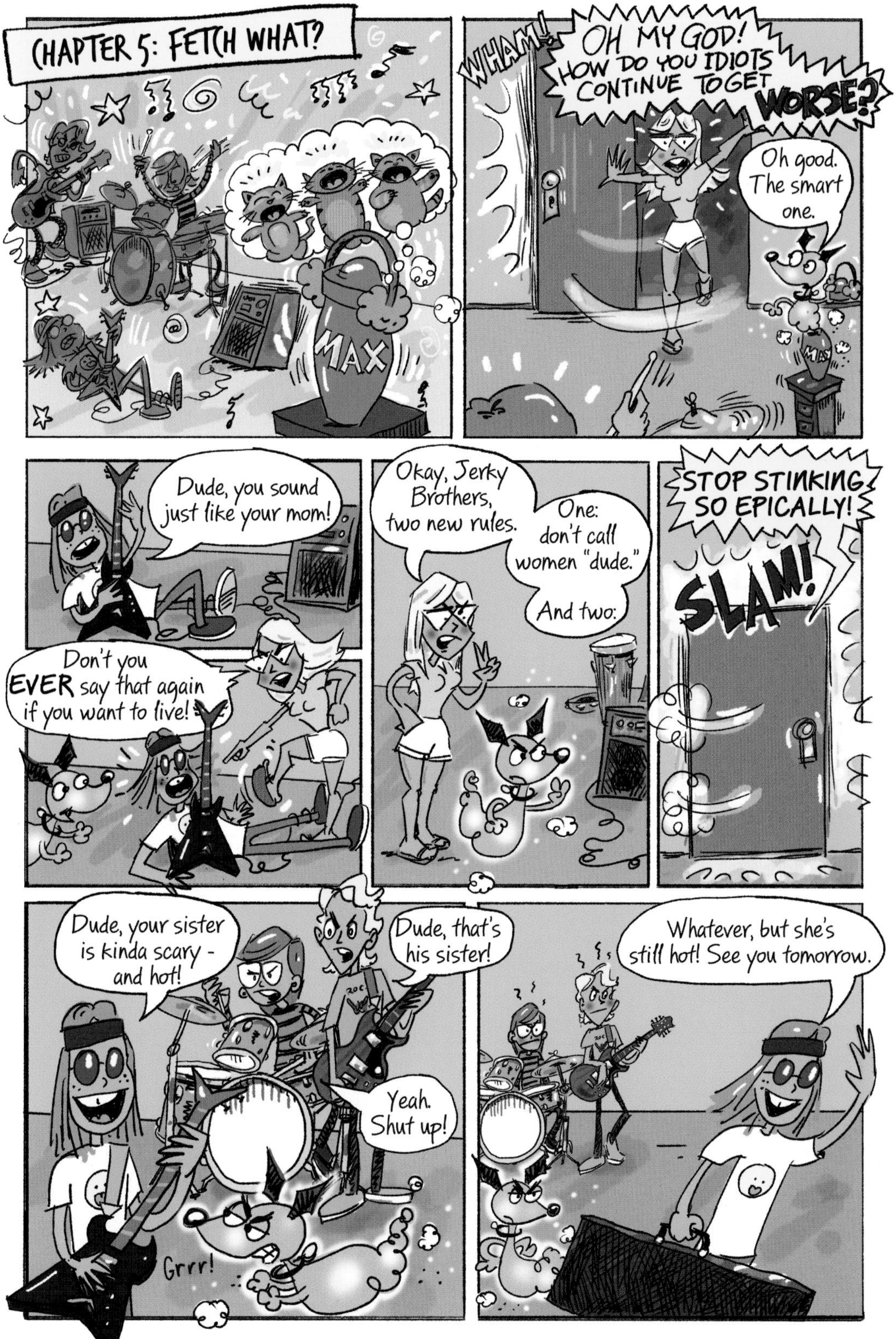
CHAPTER 5: FETCH WHAT?
MAX
WHAM!
OH MY GOD! HOW DO YOU IDIOTS CONTINUE TO GET WORSE?
Oh good. The smart one.
Dude, you sound just like your mom!
Don't you EVER say that again if you want to live!
Okay, Jerky Brothers, two new rules.
One: don't call women "dude."
And two:
STOP STINKING SO EPICALLY!
SLAM!
Dude, your sister is kinda scary - and hot!
Dude, that's his sister!
Yeah. Shut up!
Grrr!
Whatever, but she's still hot! See you tomorrow.

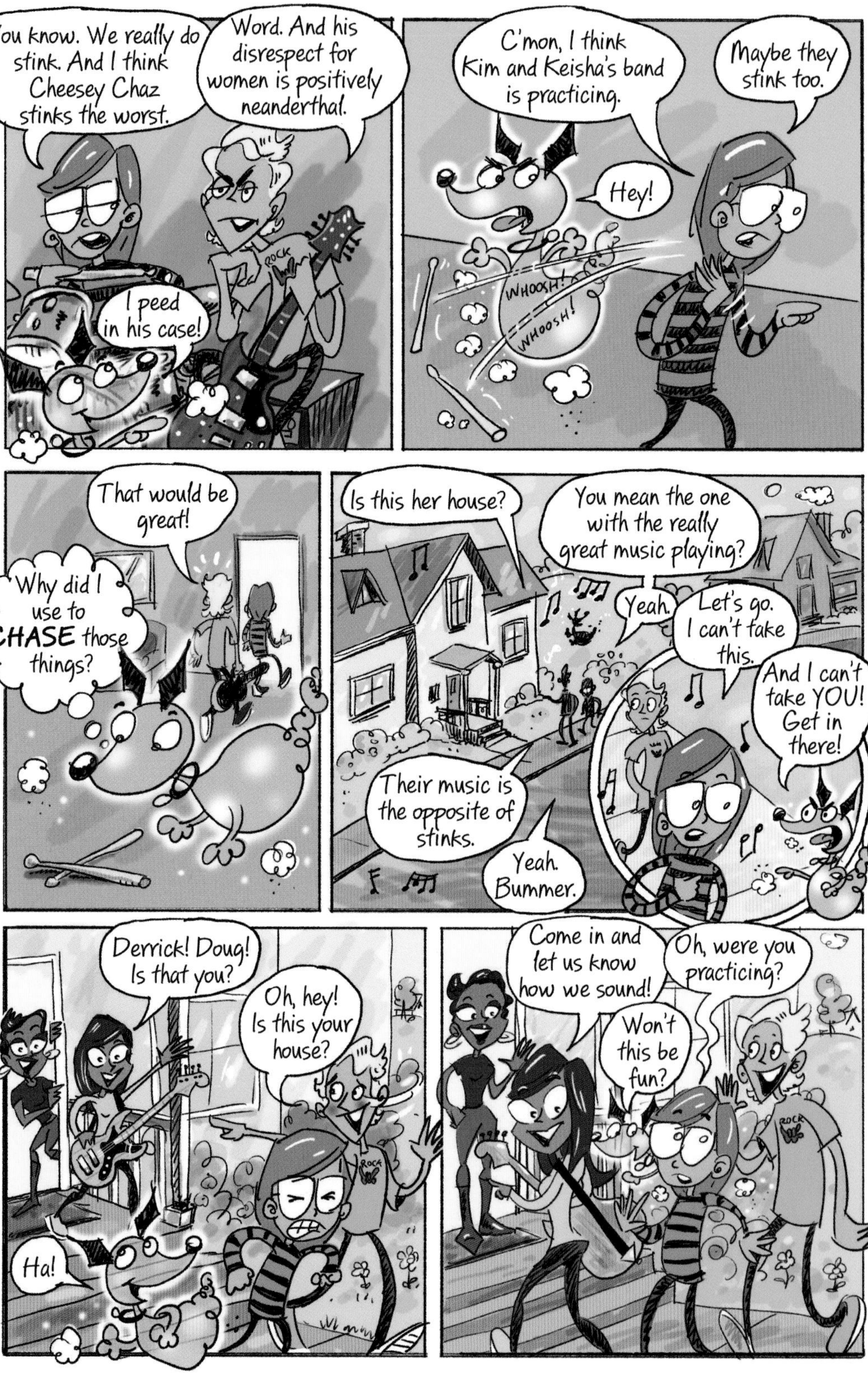
You know. We really do stink. And I think Cheesey Chaz stinks the worst.
Word. And his disrespect for women is positively neanderthal.
I peed in his case!
ROCK
C'mon, I think Kim and Keisha's band is practicing.
Maybe they stink too.
Hey!
WHOOSH!
WHOOSH!
That would be great!
Why did I use to CHASE those things?
Is this her house?
You mean the one with the really great music playing?
Yeah.
Let's go. I can't take this.
And I can't take YOU! Get in there!
Their music is the opposite of stinks.
Yeah. Bummer.
Derrick! Doug! Is that you?
Oh, hey! Is this your house?
Ha!
ROCK
Come in and let us know how we sound!
Oh, were you practicing?
Won't this be fun?
ROCK

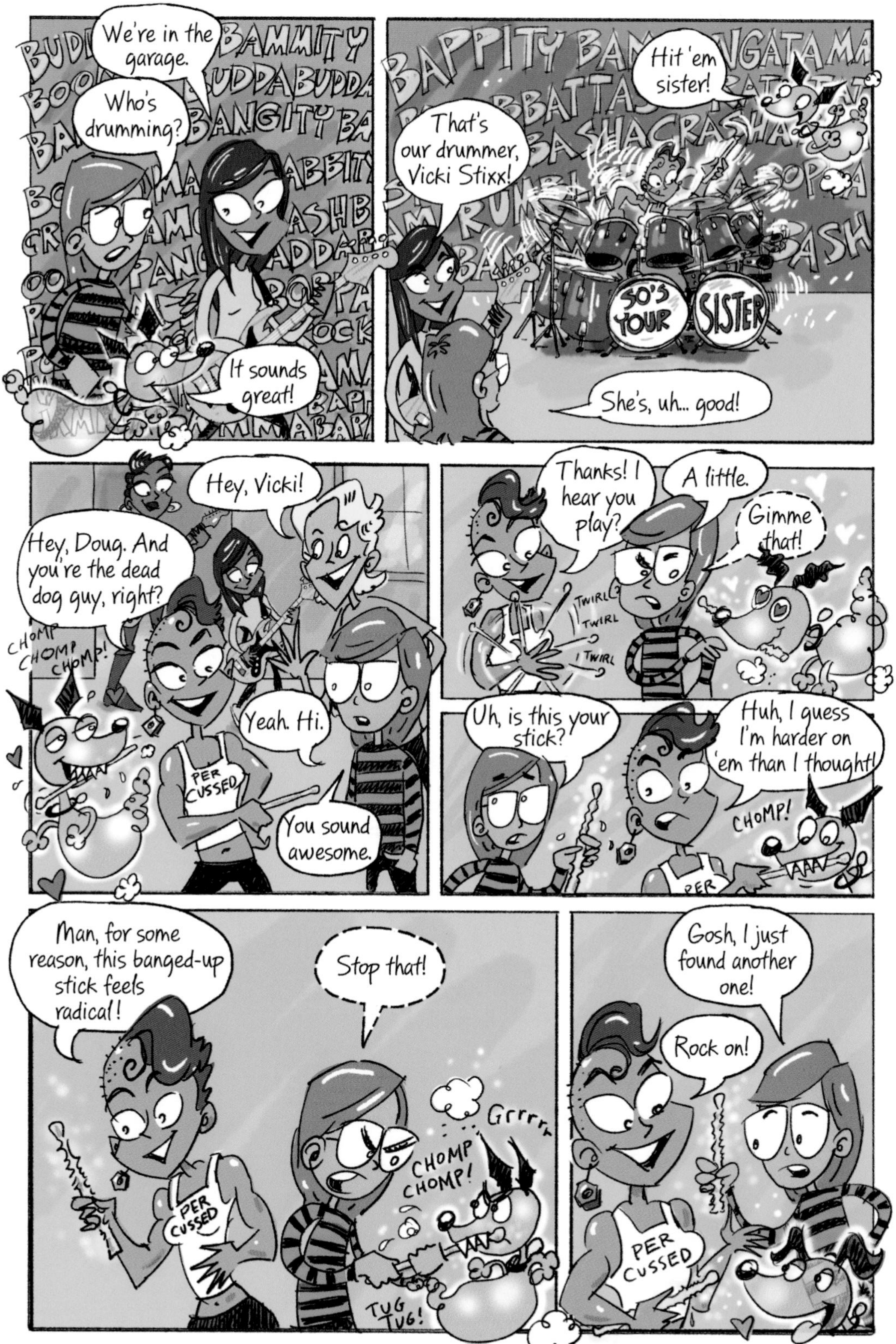
We're in the garage.
Who's drumming?
BAMMITY
BUDDABUDDA
BANGITY
It sounds great!
That's our drummer, Vicki Stixx!
Hit 'em sister!
BAPPITY
SO'S YOUR SISTER
She's, uh... good!
Hey, Vicki!
Hey, Doug. And you're the dead dog guy, right?
CHOMP CHOMP CHOMP!
Yeah. Hi.
PER CUSSED
You sound awesome.
Thanks! I hear you play?
A little.
Gimme that!
TWIRL
TWIRL
TWIRL
Uh, is this your stick?
Huh, I guess I'm harder on 'em than I thought!
CHOMP!
Man, for some reason, this banged-up stick feels radical!
Stop that!
Grrrrr
CHOMP CHOMP!
TUG TUG!
Gosh, I just found another one!
Rock on!

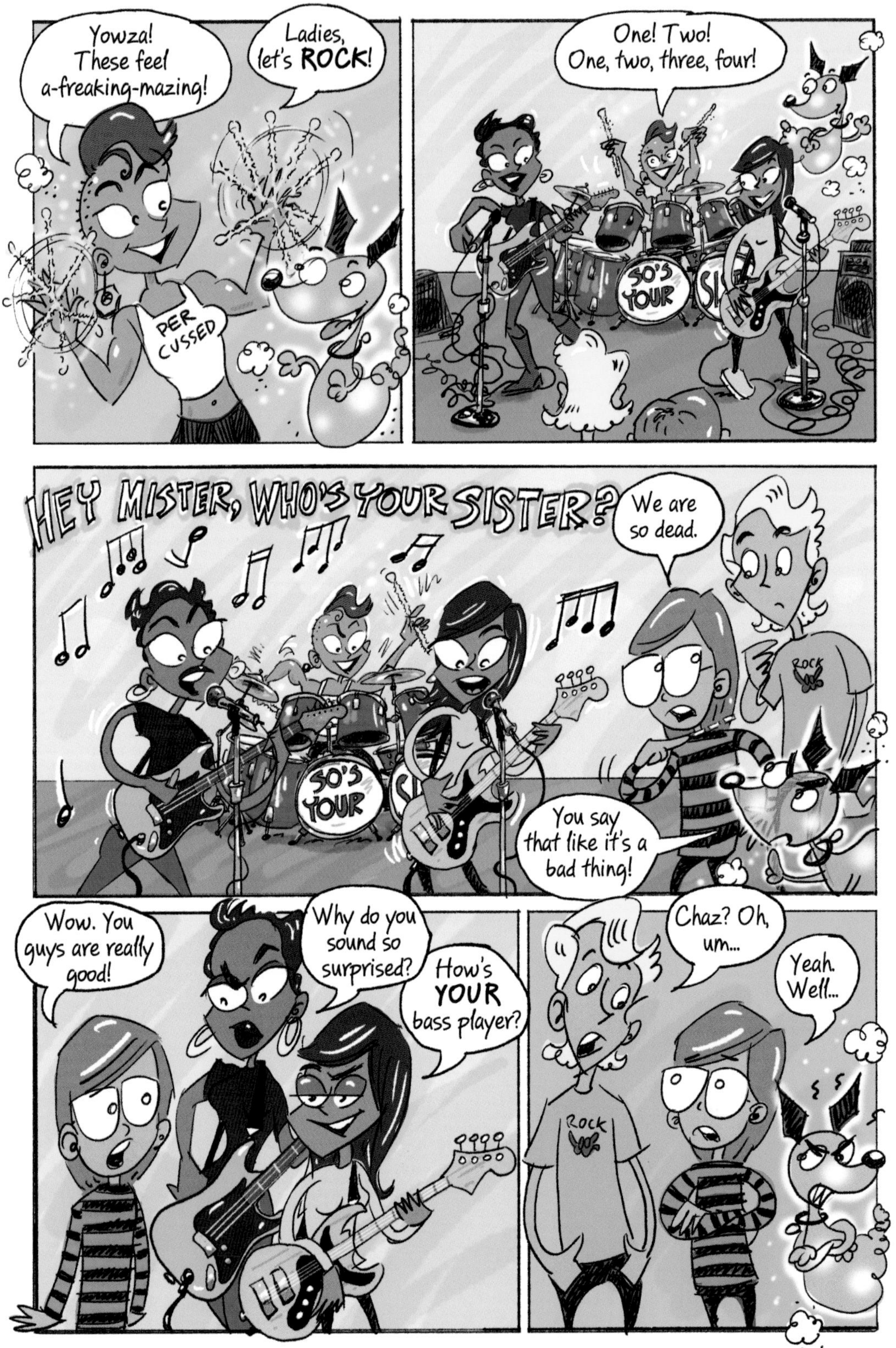
Yowza! These feel a-freaking-mazing!
Ladies, let's **ROCK**!
PER CUSSED
One! Two! One, two, three, four!
50'S YOUR
HEY MISTER, WHO'S YOUR SISTER?
We are so dead.
ROCK
You say that like it's a bad thing!
Wow. You guys are really good!
Why do you sound so surprised?
How's **YOUR** bass player?
Chaz? Oh, um...
Yeah. Well...
ROCK

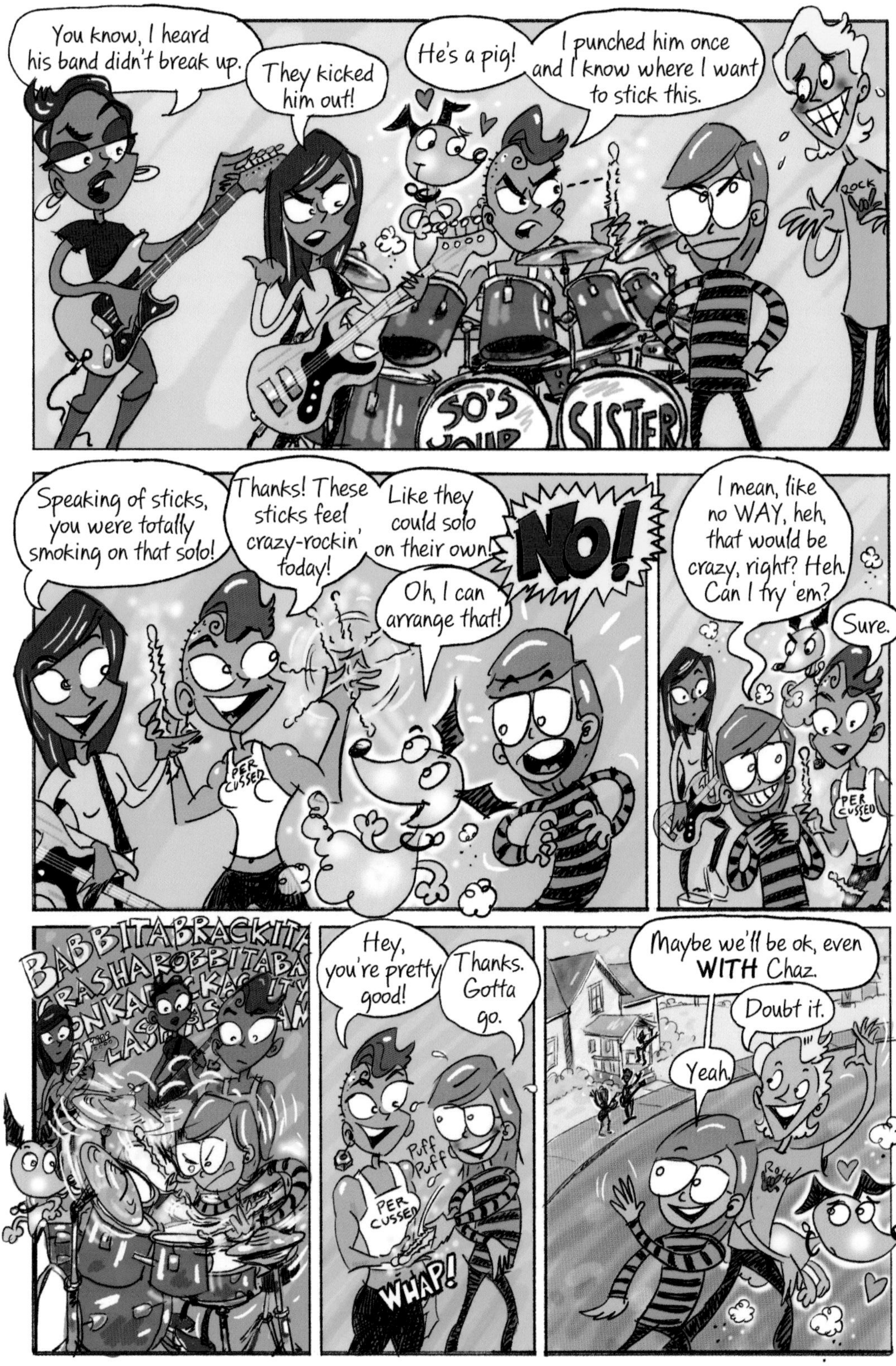
You know, I heard his band didn't break up.
They kicked him out!
He's a pig!
I punched him once and I know where I want to stick this.
ROCK
SO'S
SISTER
Speaking of sticks, you were totally smoking on that solo!
Thanks! These sticks feel crazy-rockin' today!
Like they could solo on their own!
NO!
Oh, I can arrange that!
PER CUSSED
I mean, like no WAY, heh, that would be crazy, right? Heh. Can I try 'em?
Sure.
PER CUSSED
BABBITABRACKITA
CRASHAROBBITABA
Hey, you're pretty good!
Thanks. Gotta go.
Puff Puff
PER CUSSED
WHAP!
Maybe we'll be ok, even WITH Chaz.
Doubt it.
Yeah.

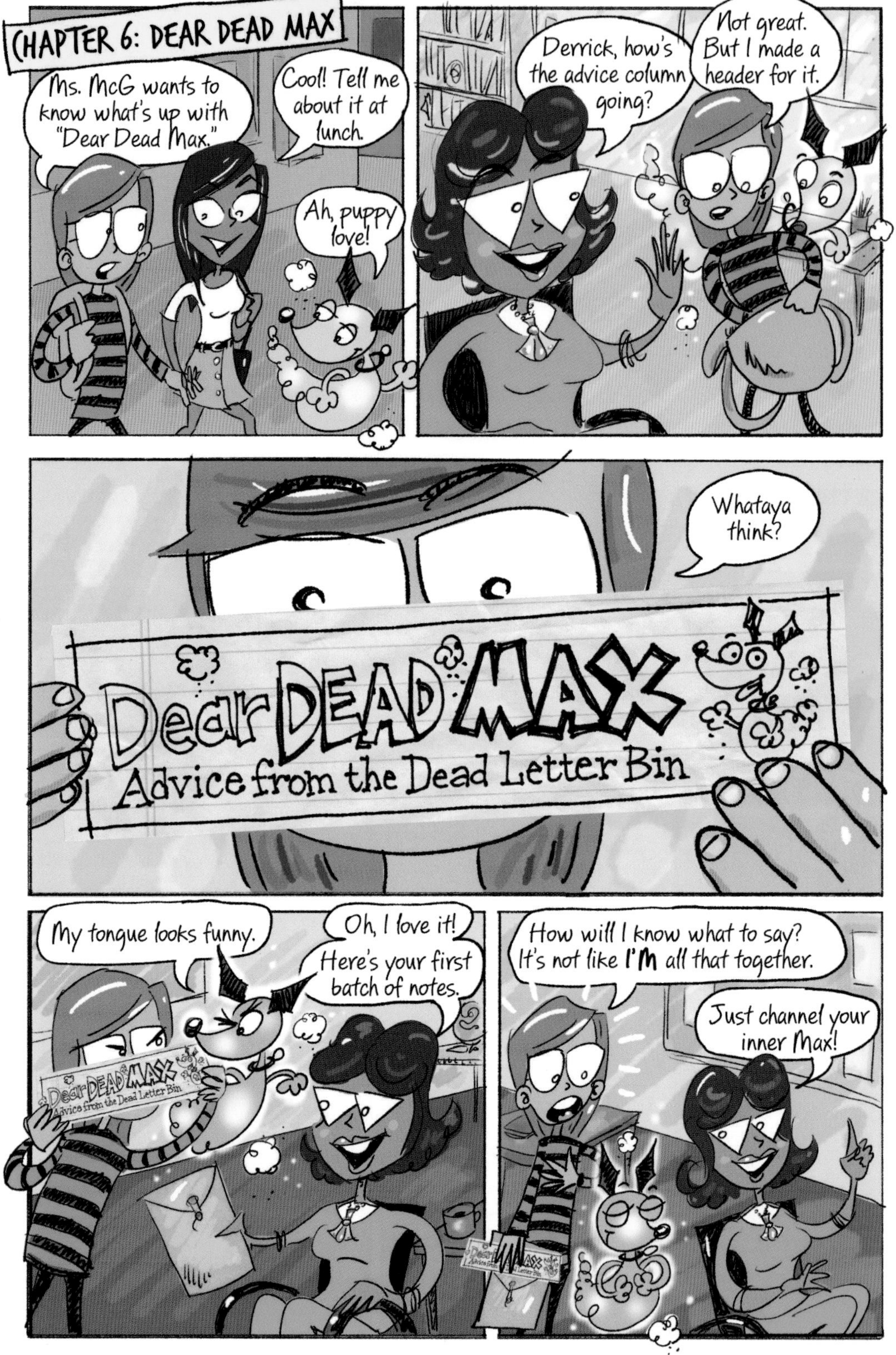
CHAPTER 6: DEAR DEAD MAX
Ms. McG wants to know what's up with "Dear Dead Max."
Cool! Tell me about it at lunch.
Ah, puppy love!
Derrick, how's the advice column going?
Not great. But I made a header for it.
Whataya think?
Dear DEAD MAX
Advice from the Dead Letter Bin
My tongue looks funny.
Oh, I love it!
Here's your first batch of notes.
How will I know what to say? It's not like I'M all that together.
Just channel your inner Max!

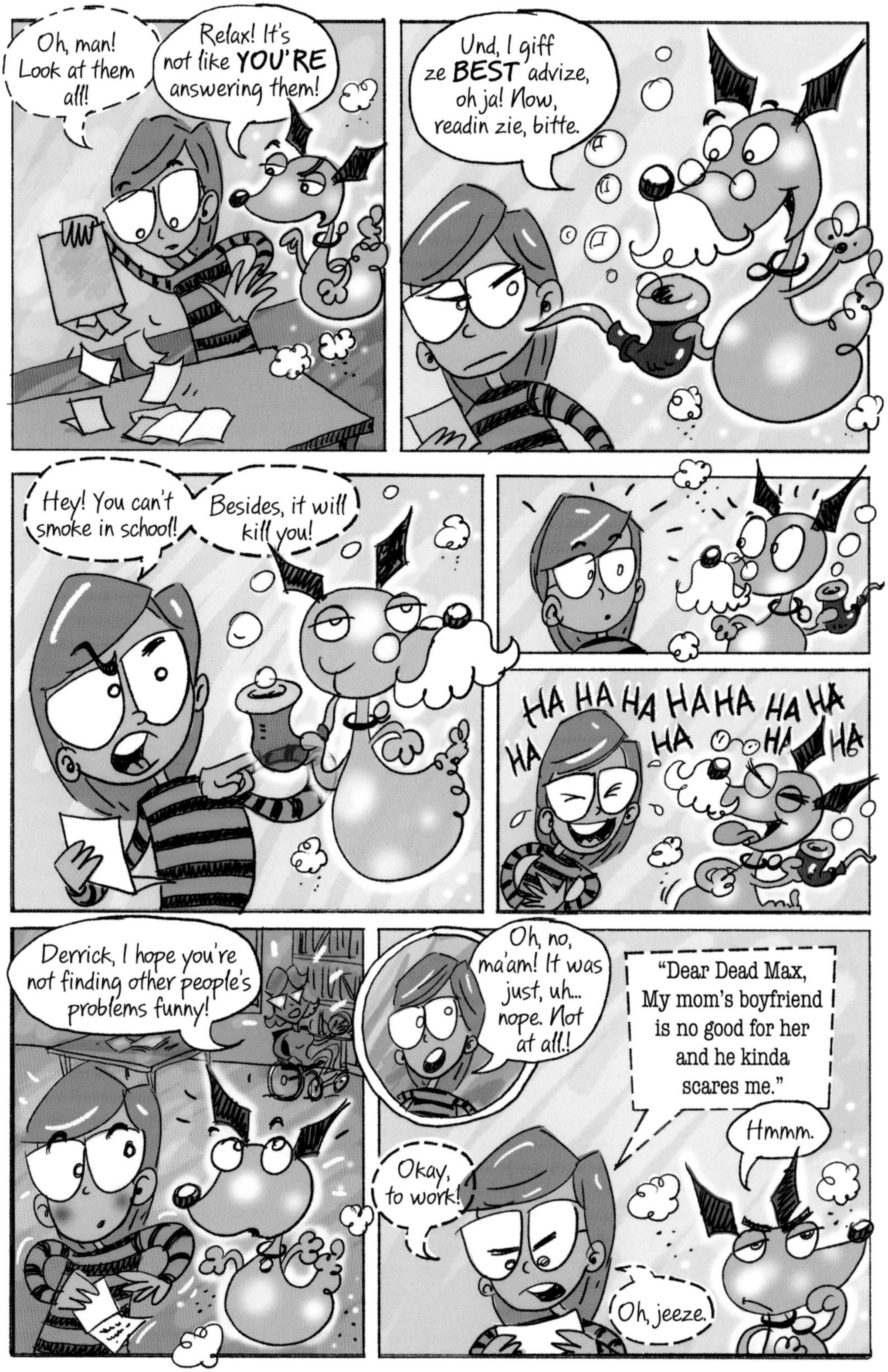

Oh, man! Look at them all!
Relax! It's not like YOU'RE answering them!
Und, I giff ze BEST advize, oh ja! Now, readin zie, bitte.
Hey! You can't smoke in school!
Besides, it will kill you!
HA HA HA HA HA HA HA HA HA HA HA HA
Derrick, I hope you're not finding other people's problems funny!
Oh, no, ma'am! It was just, uh... nope. Not at all.!
"Dear Dead Max, My mom's boyfriend is no good for her and he kinda scares me."
Hmmm.
Okay, to work!
Oh, jeeze.

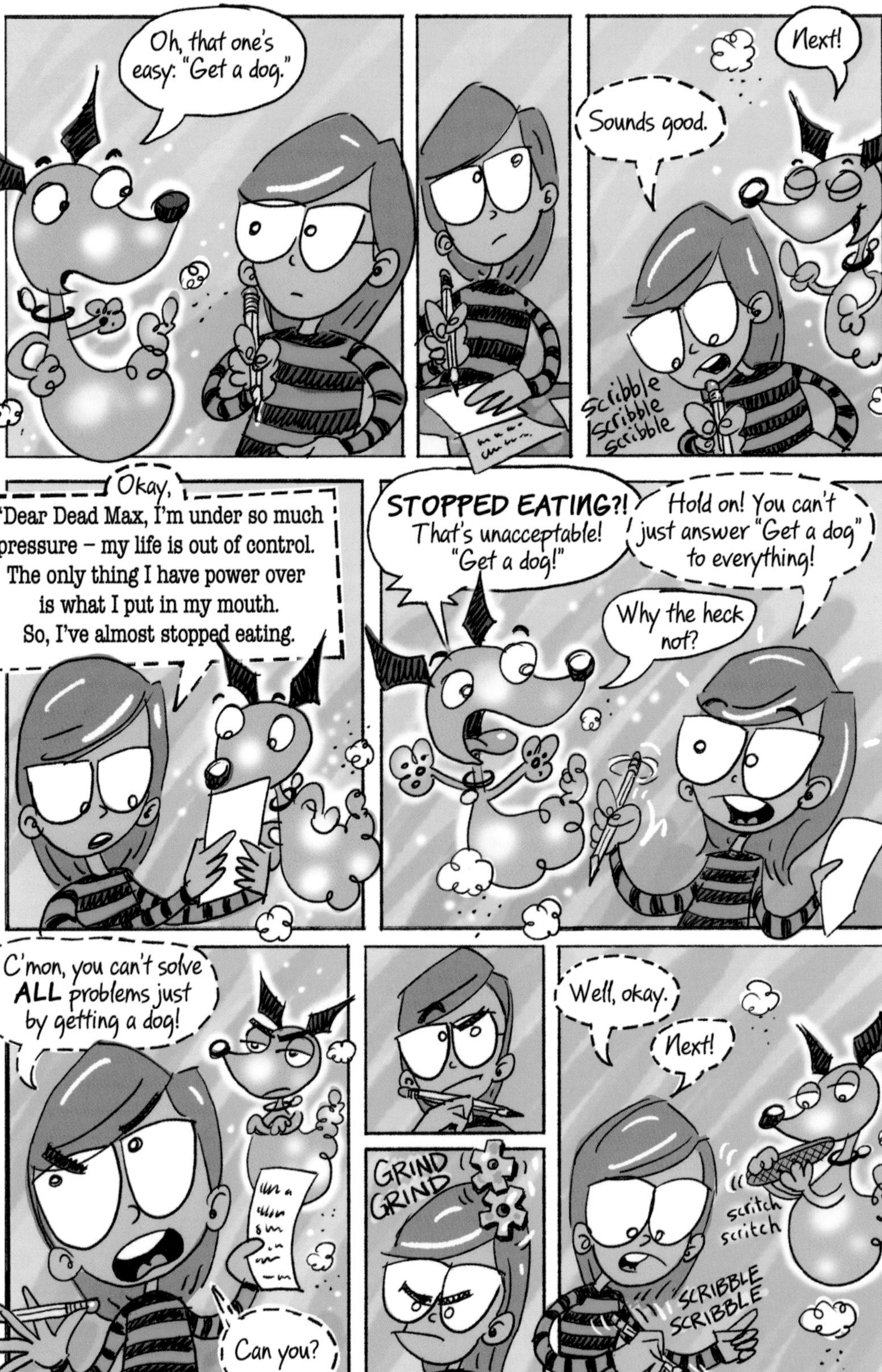
Oh, that one's easy: "Get a dog."
Sounds good.
Next!
scribble scribble scribble
Okay,
"Dear Dead Max, I'm under so much pressure – my life is out of control. The only thing I have power over is what I put in my mouth. So, I've almost stopped eating.
STOPPED EATING?! That's unacceptable! "Get a dog!"
Hold on! You can't just answer "Get a dog" to everything!
Why the heck not?
C'mon, you can't solve ALL problems just by getting a dog!
Can you?
GRIND GRIND
Well, okay.
Next!
scritch scritch
SCRIBBLE SCRIBBLE

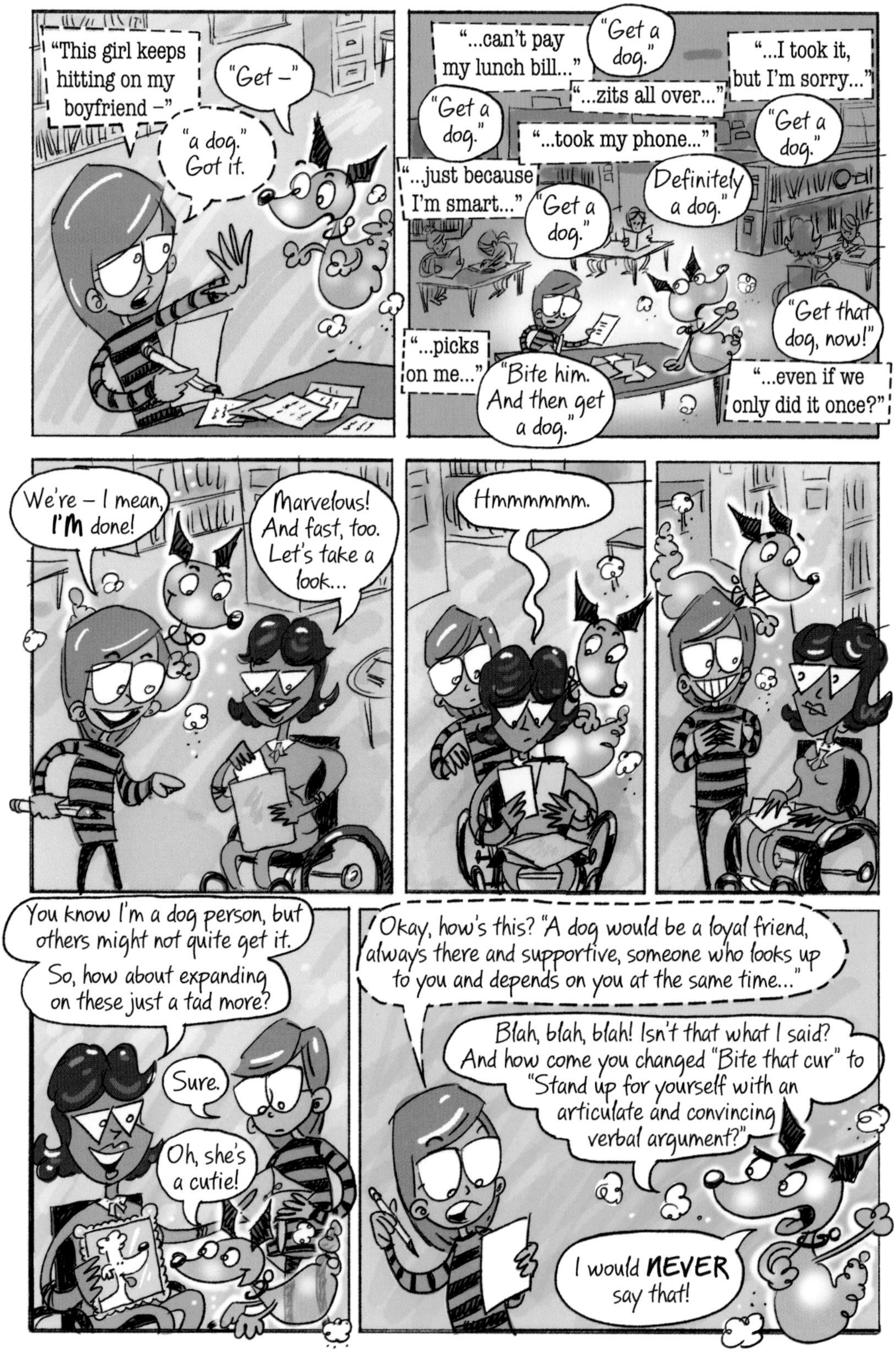
"This girl keeps hitting on my boyfriend –"
"Get –"
"a dog." Got it.
"...can't pay my lunch bill..."
"Get a dog."
"...I took it, but I'm sorry..."
"...zits all over..."
"Get a dog."
"Get a dog."
"...took my phone..."
"...just because I'm smart..."
"Get a dog."
Definitely a dog.
"Get that dog, now!"
"...picks on me..."
"Bite him. And then get a dog."
"...even if we only did it once?"
We're – I mean, I'M done!
Marvelous! And fast, too. Let's take a look...
Hmmmmmm.
You know I'm a dog person, but others might not quite get it.
So, how about expanding on these just a tad more?
Sure.
Oh, she's a cutie!
Okay, how's this? "A dog would be a loyal friend, always there and supportive, someone who looks up to you and depends on you at the same time..."
Blah, blah, blah! Isn't that what I said? And how come you changed "Bite that cur" to "Stand up for yourself with an articulate and convincing verbal argument?"
I would NEVER say that!

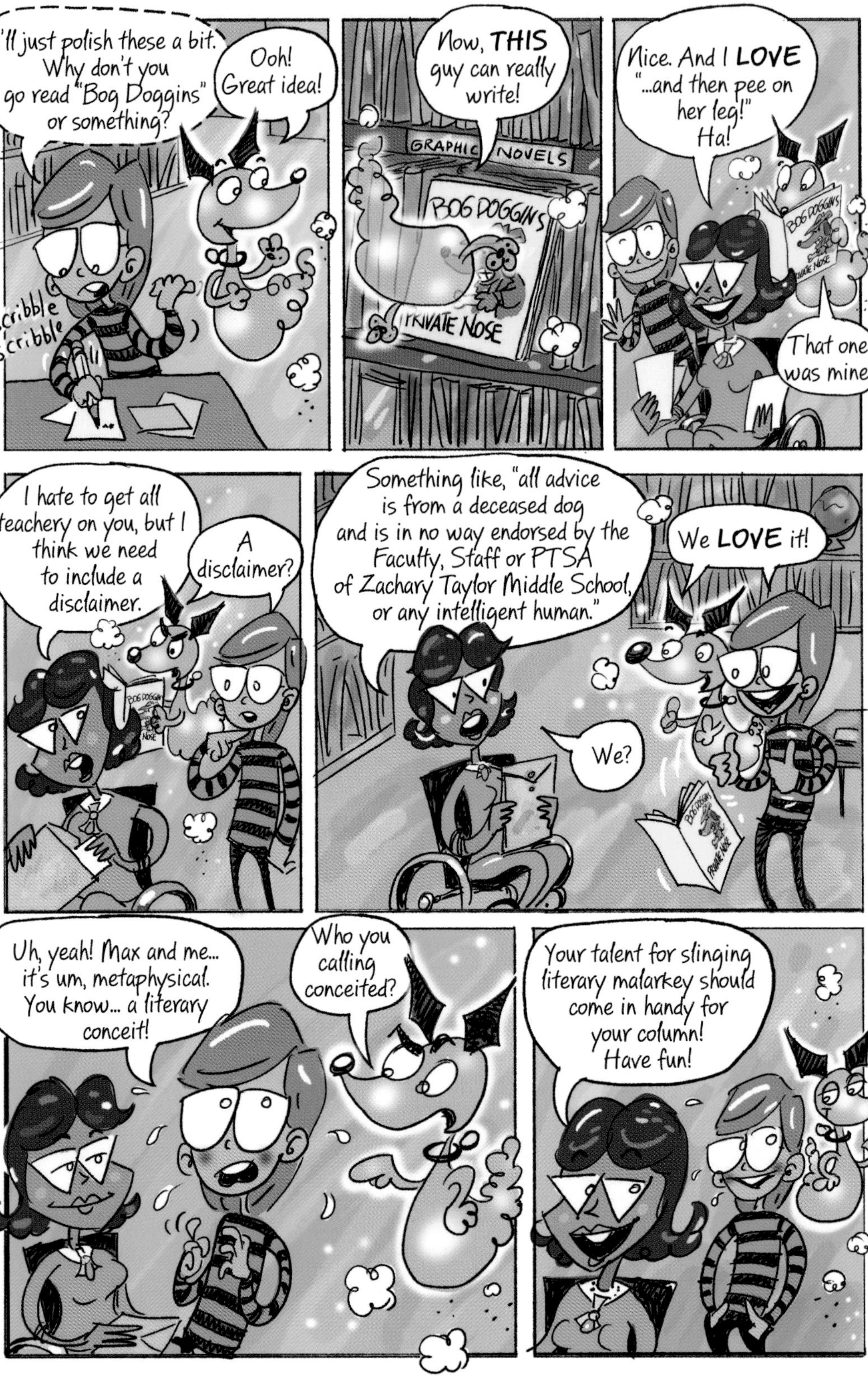

I'll just polish these a bit. Why don't you go read "Bog Doggins" or something?
Ooh! Great idea!
scribble scribble
Now, THIS guy can really write!
GRAPHIC NOVELS
BOG DOGGINS PRIVATE NOSE
Nice. And I LOVE "...and then pee on her leg!" Ha!
That one was mine.
I hate to get all teachery on you, but I think we need to include a disclaimer.
A disclaimer?
Something like, "all advice is from a deceased dog and is in no way endorsed by the Faculty, Staff or PTSA of Zachary Taylor Middle School, or any intelligent human."
We LOVE it!
We?
Uh, yeah! Max and me... it's um, metaphysical. You know... a literary conceit!
Who you calling conceited?
Your talent for slinging literary malarkey should come in handy for your column! Have fun!

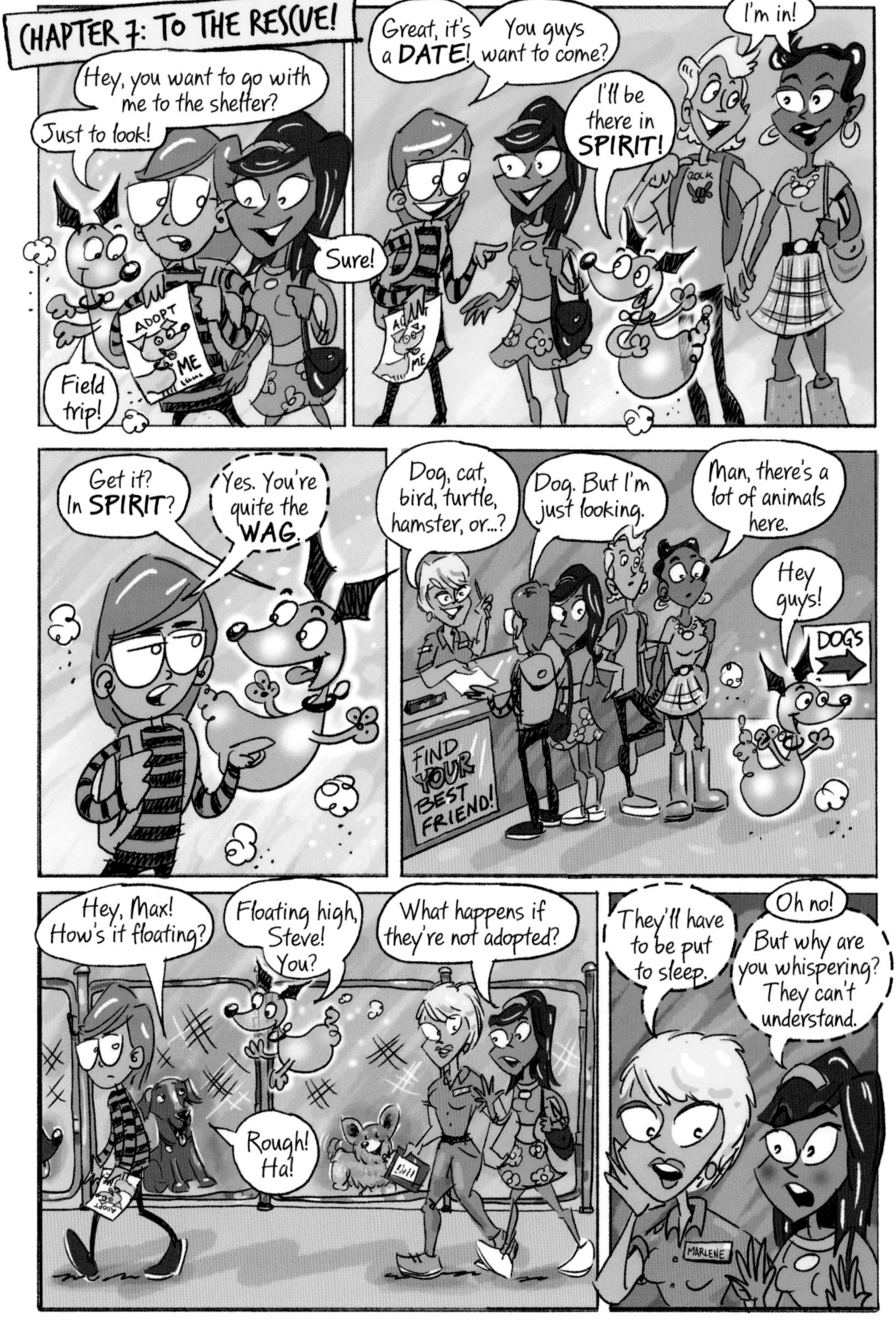
CHAPTER 7: TO THE RESCUE!
Hey, you want to go with me to the shelter?
Just to look!
Sure!
ADOPT ME
Field trip!
Great, it's a DATE!
You guys want to come?
I'll be there in SPIRIT!
I'm in!
ROCK
Get it? In SPIRIT?
Yes. You're quite the WAG.
Dog, cat, bird, turtle, hamster, or...?
Dog. But I'm just looking.
Man, there's a lot of animals here.
Hey guys!
DOGS
FIND YOUR BEST FRIEND!
Hey, Max! How's it floating?
Floating high, Steve! You?
Rough! Ha!
What happens if they're not adopted?
They'll have to be put to sleep.
Oh no!
But why are you whispering? They can't understand.
MARLENE

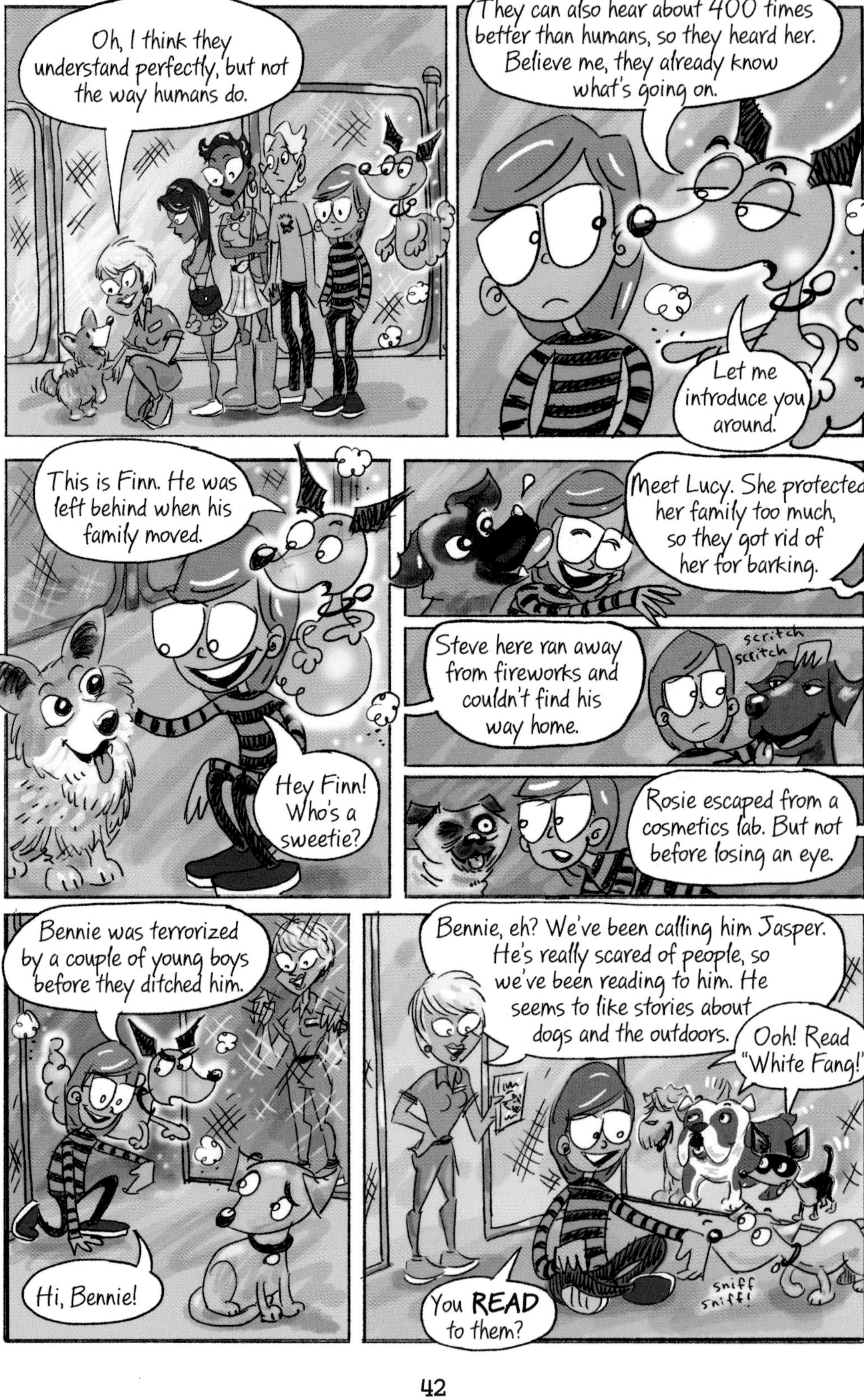

Oh, I think they understand perfectly, but not the way humans do.
They can also hear about 400 times better than humans, so they heard her. Believe me, they already know what's going on.
Let me introduce you around.
This is Finn. He was left behind when his family moved.
Hey Finn! Who's a sweetie?
Meet Lucy. She protected her family too much, so they got rid of her for barking.
Steve here ran away from fireworks and couldn't find his way home.
scritch scritch
Rosie escaped from a cosmetics lab. But not before losing an eye.
Bennie was terrorized by a couple of young boys before they ditched him.
Hi, Bennie!
Bennie, eh? We've been calling him Jasper. He's really scared of people, so we've been reading to him. He seems to like stories about dogs and the outdoors.
Ooh! Read "White Fang!"
You **READ** to them?
sniff sniff!

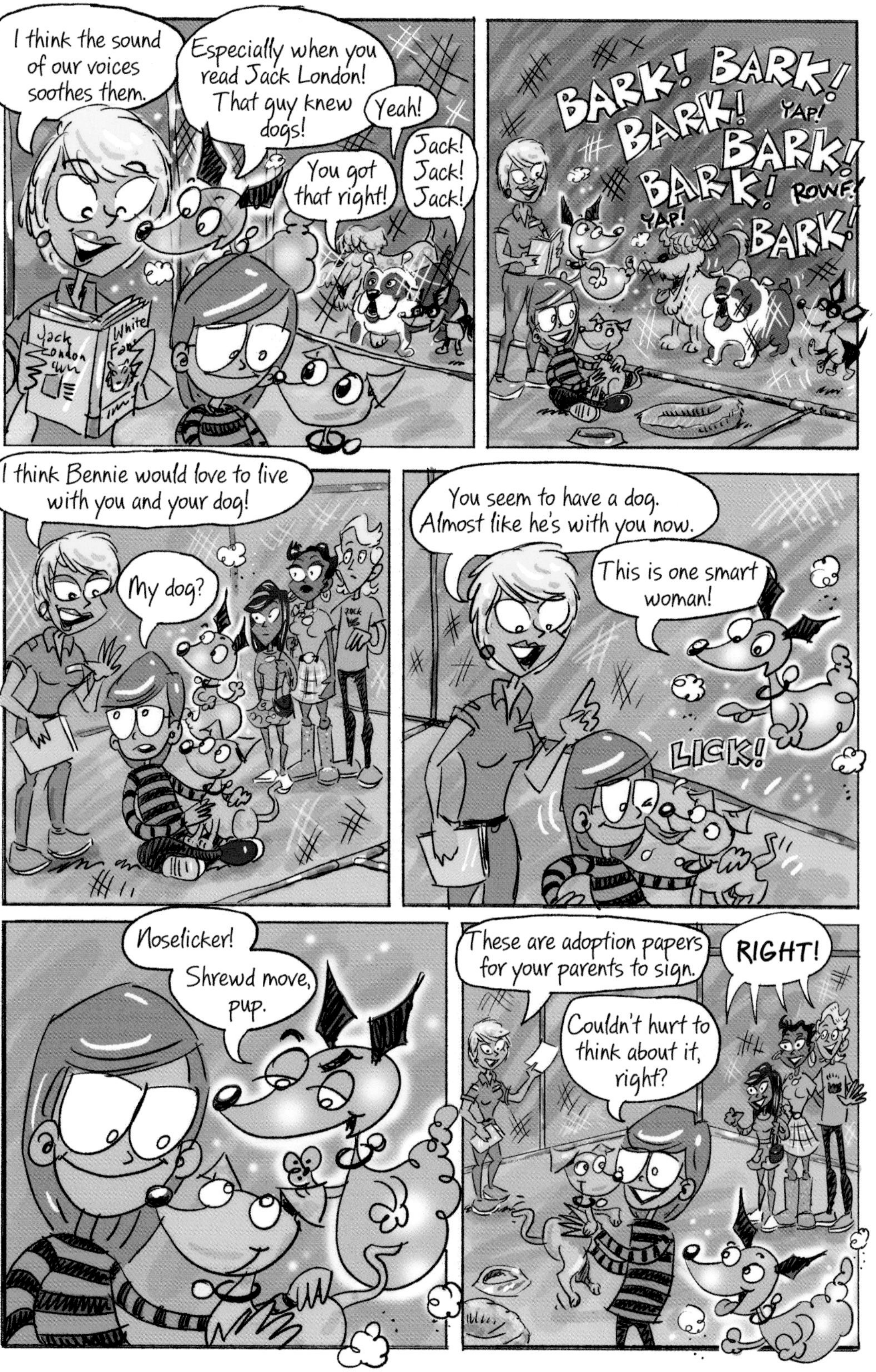
I think the sound of our voices soothes them.
Especially when you read Jack London! That guy knew dogs!
Yeah!
You got that right!
Jack! Jack! Jack!
Jack London
White Fang
BARK! BARK! BARK! YAP! BARK! BARK! ROWF! YAP! BARK!
I think Bennie would love to live with you and your dog!
My dog?
You seem to have a dog. Almost like he's with you now.
This is one smart woman!
LICK!
Noselicker!
Shrewd move, pup.
These are adoption papers for your parents to sign.
RIGHT!
Couldn't hurt to think about it, right?

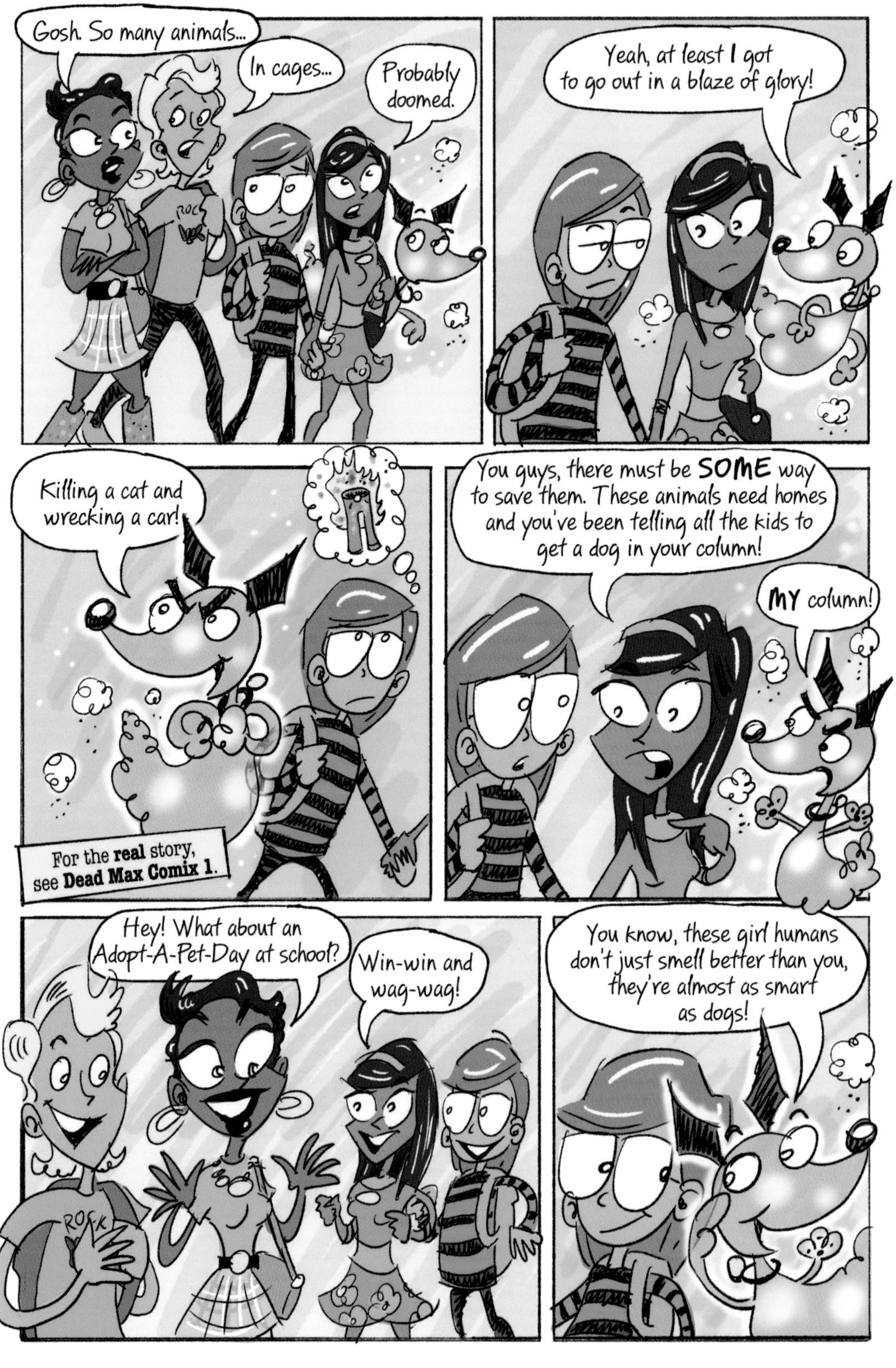
Gosh. So many animals...
In cages...
Probably doomed.
Yeah, at least I got to go out in a blaze of glory!
Killing a cat and wrecking a car!
For the real story, see Dead Max Comix 1.
You guys, there must be SOME way to save them. These animals need homes and you've been telling all the kids to get a dog in your column!
MY column!
Hey! What about an Adopt-A-Pet-Day at school?
Win-win and wag-wag!
You know, these girl humans don't just smell better than you, they're almost as smart as dogs!

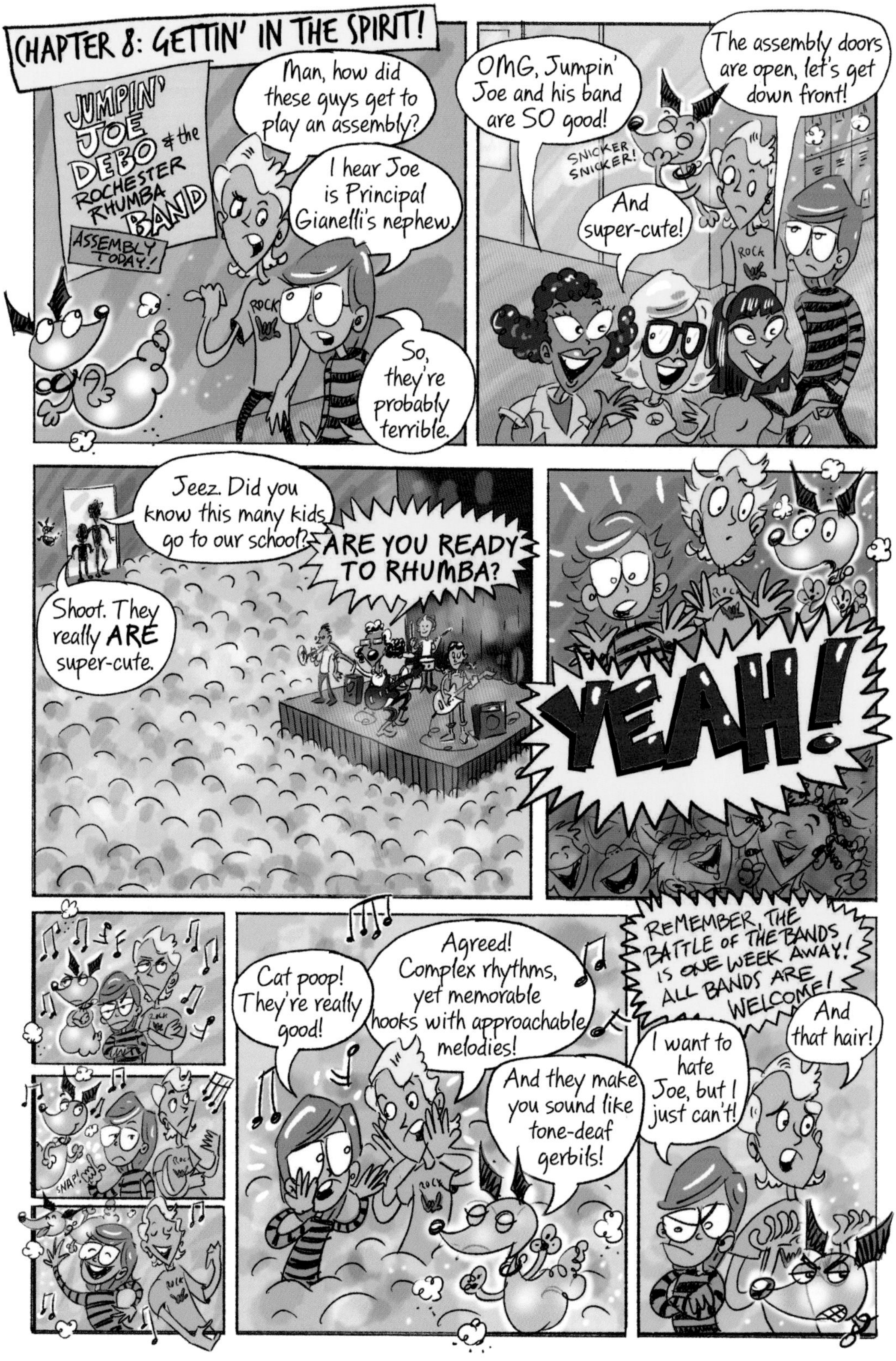
CHAPTER 8: GETTIN' IN THE SPIRIT!
JUMPIN' JOE DEBO & the ROCHESTER RHUMBA BAND
ASSEMBLY TODAY!
Man, how did these guys get to play an assembly?
I hear Joe is Principal Gianelli's nephew.
So, they're probably terrible.
OMG, Jumpin' Joe and his band are SO good!
SNICKER SNICKER!
The assembly doors are open, let's get down front!
And super-cute!
Jeez. Did you know this many kids go to our school?
ARE YOU READY TO RHUMBA?
Shoot. They really ARE super-cute.
YEAH!
SNAP!
Cat poop! They're really good!
Agreed! Complex rhythms, yet memorable hooks with approachable melodies!
And they make you sound like tone-deaf gerbils!
REMEMBER, THE BATTLE OF THE BANDS IS ONE WEEK AWAY! ALL BANDS ARE WELCOME!
I want to hate Joe, but I just can't!
And that hair!

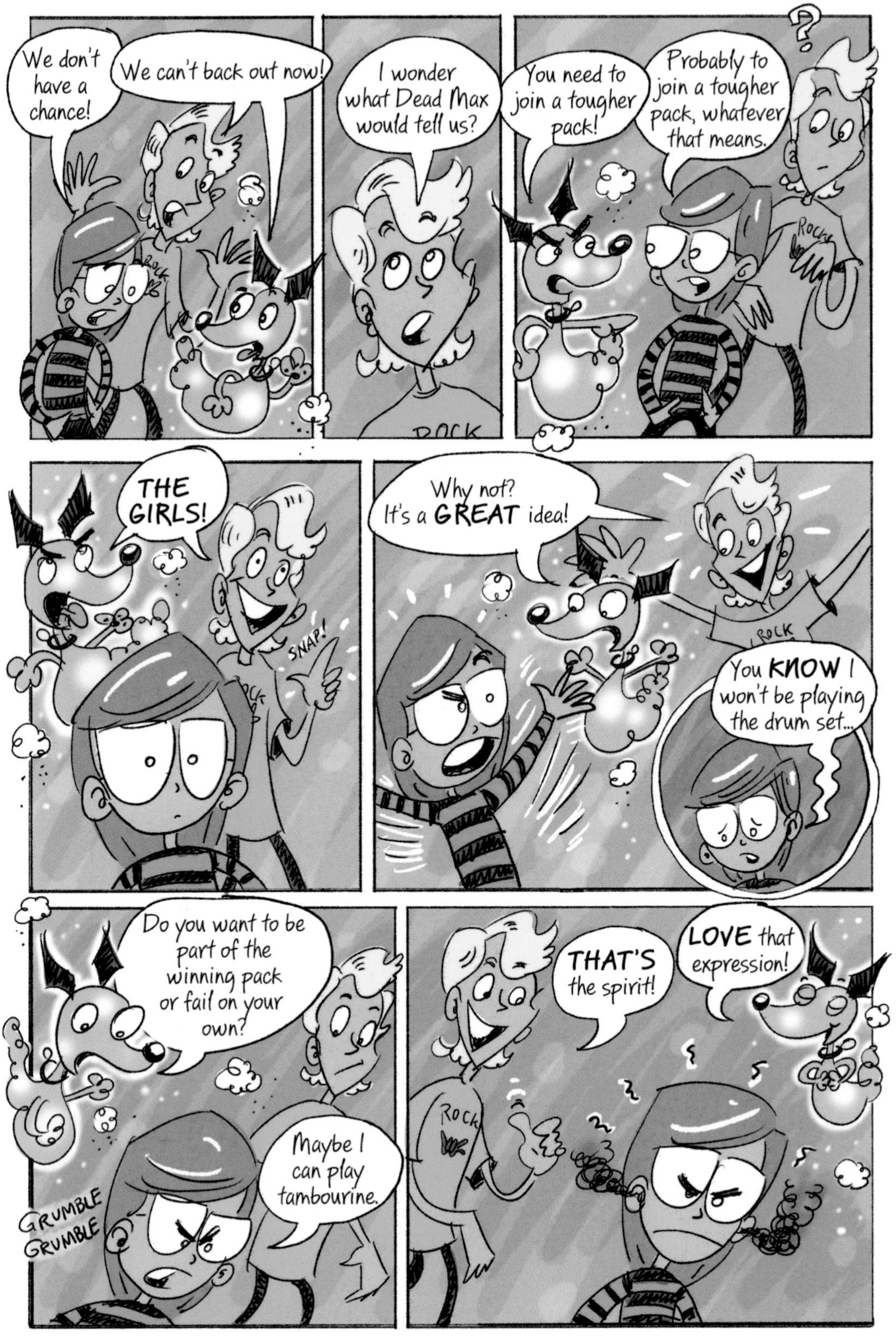
We don't have a chance!
We can't back out now!
ROCK
I wonder what Dead Max would tell us?
ROCK
You need to join a tougher pack!
Probably to join a tougher pack, whatever that means.
?
ROCK
THE GIRLS!
SNAP!
ROCK
Why not? It's a GREAT idea!
ROCK
You KNOW I won't be playing the drum set...
Do you want to be part of the winning pack or fail on your own?
GRUMBLE GRUMBLE
Maybe I can play tambourine.
THAT'S the spirit!
LOVE that expression!
ROCK

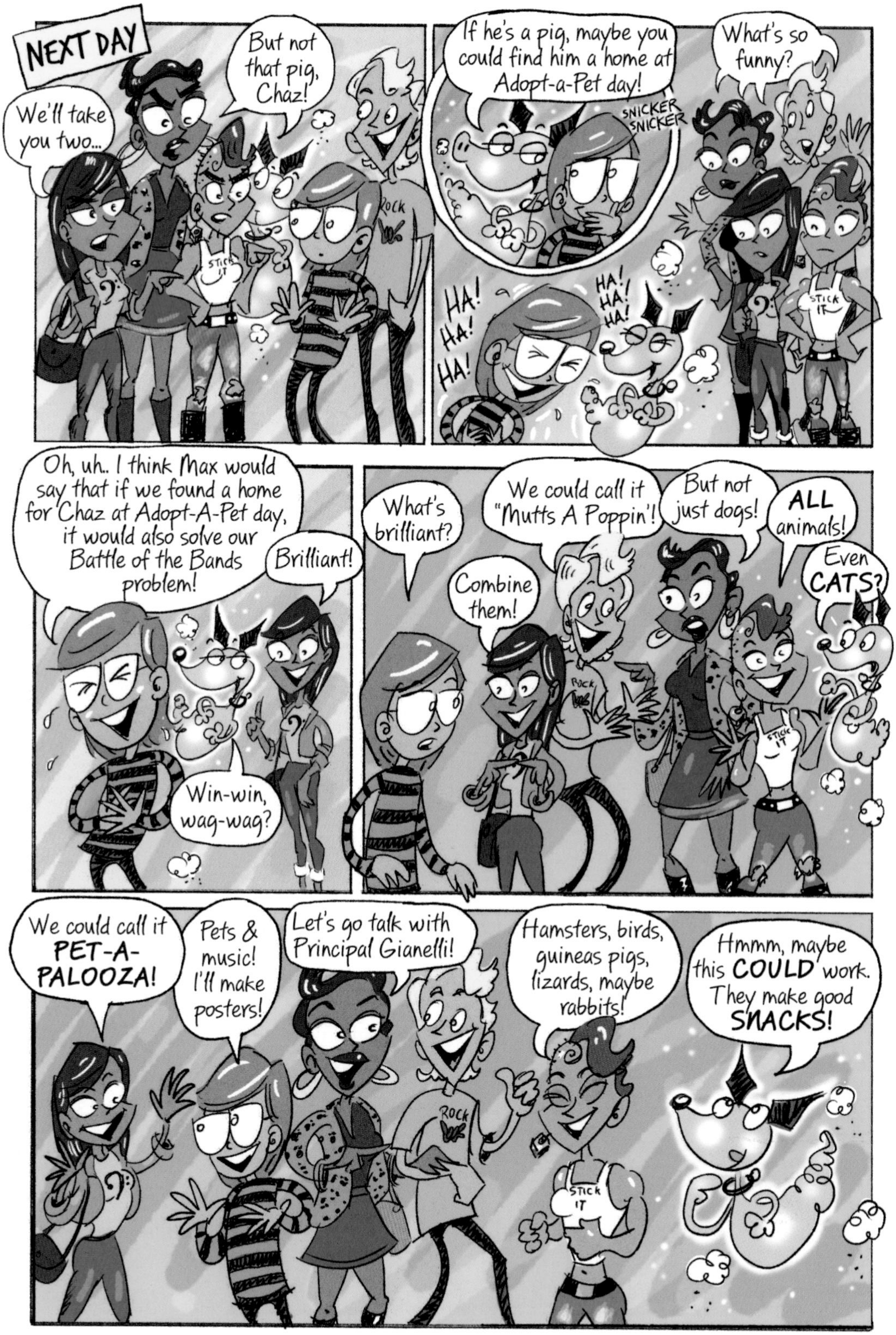
NEXT DAY
We'll take you two...
But not that pig, Chaz!
If he's a pig, maybe you could find him a home at Adopt-a-Pet day!
SNICKER SNICKER
What's so funny?
HA! HA! HA!
HA! HA! HA!
Oh, uh.. I think Max would say that if we found a home for Chaz at Adopt-A-Pet day, it would also solve our Battle of the Bands problem!
Brilliant!
Win-win, wag-wag?
What's brilliant?
Combine them!
We could call it "Mutts A Poppin'!
But not just dogs!
ALL animals!
Even CATS?
We could call it PET-A-PALOOZA!
Pets & music! I'll make posters!
Let's go talk with Principal Gianelli!
Hamsters, birds, guineas pigs, lizards, maybe rabbits!
Hmmm, maybe this COULD work. They make good SNACKS!

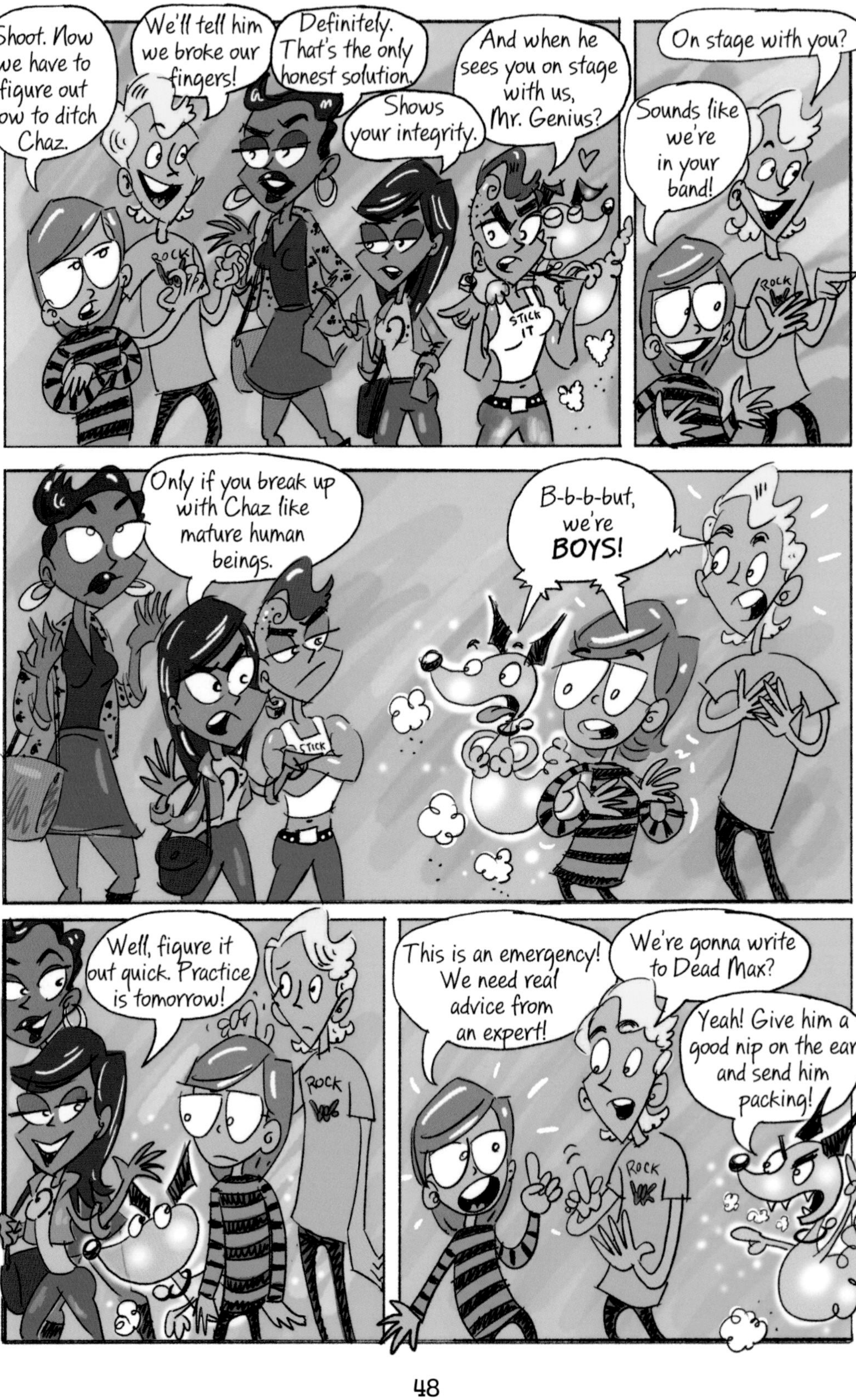
Shoot. Now we have to figure out how to ditch Chaz.
We'll tell him we broke our fingers!
Definitely. That's the only honest solution.
Shows your integrity.
And when he sees you on stage with us, Mr. Genius?
ROCK
STICK IT
On stage with you?
Sounds like we're in your band!
ROCK
Only if you break up with Chaz like mature human beings.
B-b-b-but, we're BOYS!
STICK
Well, figure it out quick. Practice is tomorrow!
ROCK
This is an emergency! We need real advice from an expert!
We're gonna write to Dead Max?
Yeah! Give him a good nip on the ear and send him packing!
ROCK

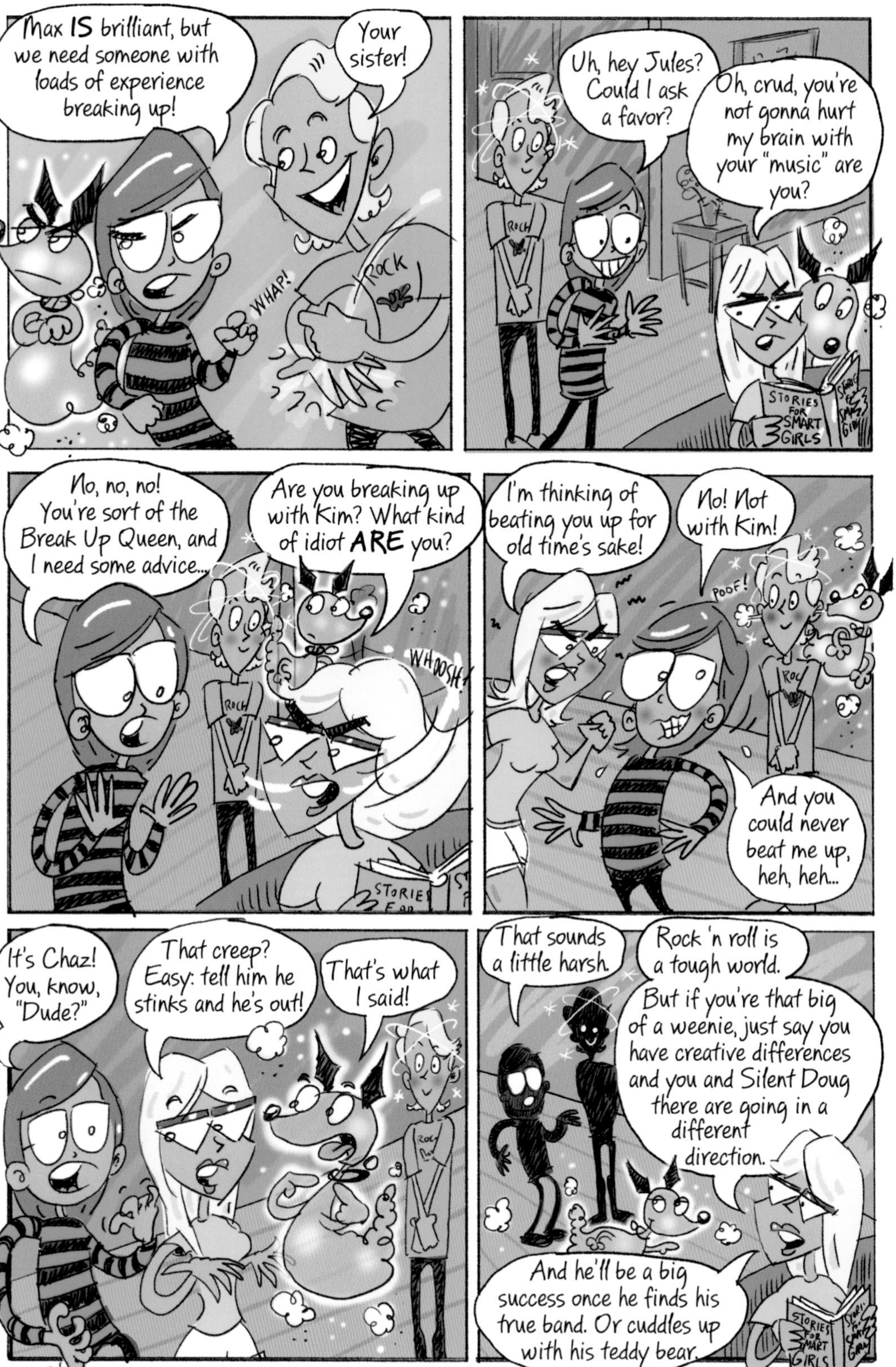
Max IS brilliant, but we need someone with loads of experience breaking up!
Your sister!
WHAP!
ROCK
Uh, hey Jules? Could I ask a favor?
Oh, crud, you're not gonna hurt my brain with your "music" are you?
STORIES FOR SMART GIRLS
No, no, no! You're sort of the Break Up Queen, and I need some advice...
Are you breaking up with Kim? What kind of idiot ARE you?
WHOOSH!
I'm thinking of beating you up for old time's sake!
No! Not with Kim!
POOF!
And you could never beat me up, heh, heh...
It's Chaz! You, know, "Dude?"
That creep? Easy: tell him he stinks and he's out!
That's what I said!
That sounds a little harsh.
Rock 'n roll is a tough world.
But if you're that big of a weenie, just say you have creative differences and you and Silent Doug there are going in a different direction.
And he'll be a big success once he finds his true band. Or cuddles up with his teddy bear.
STORIES FOR SMART GIRLS

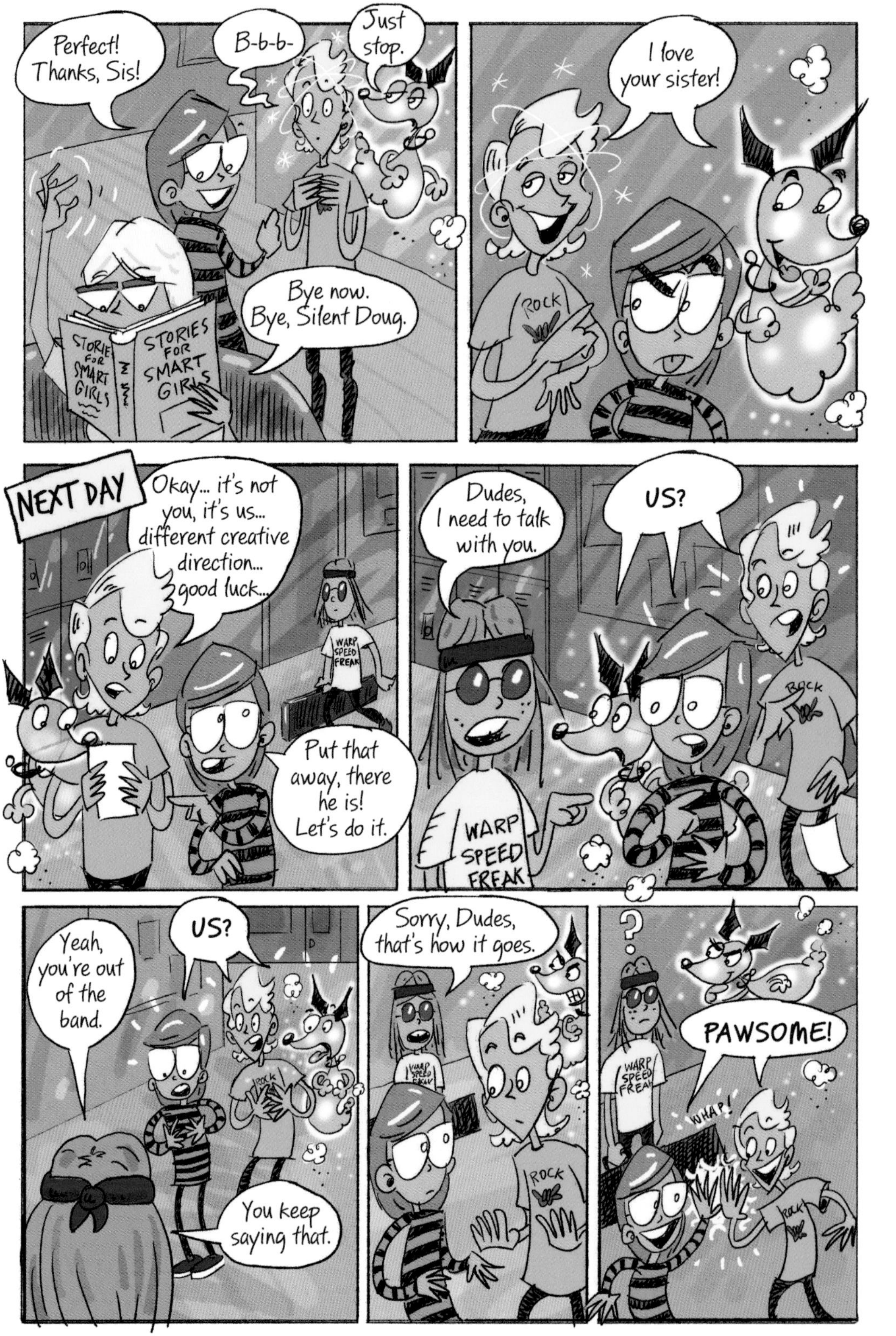
Perfect! Thanks, Sis!
B-b-b-
Just stop.
Bye now. Bye, Silent Doug.
STORIES FOR SMART GIRLS
STORIES FOR SMART GIRLS
I love your sister!
ROCK
NEXT DAY
Okay... it's not you, it's us... different creative direction... good luck...
WARP SPEED FREAK
Put that away, there he is! Let's do it.
Dudes, I need to talk with you.
US?
WARP SPEED FREAK
ROCK
Yeah, you're out of the band.
US?
ROCK
You keep saying that.
Sorry, Dudes, that's how it goes.
WARP SPEED FREAK
ROCK
?
PAWSOME!
WARP SPEED FREAK
WHAP!
ROCK

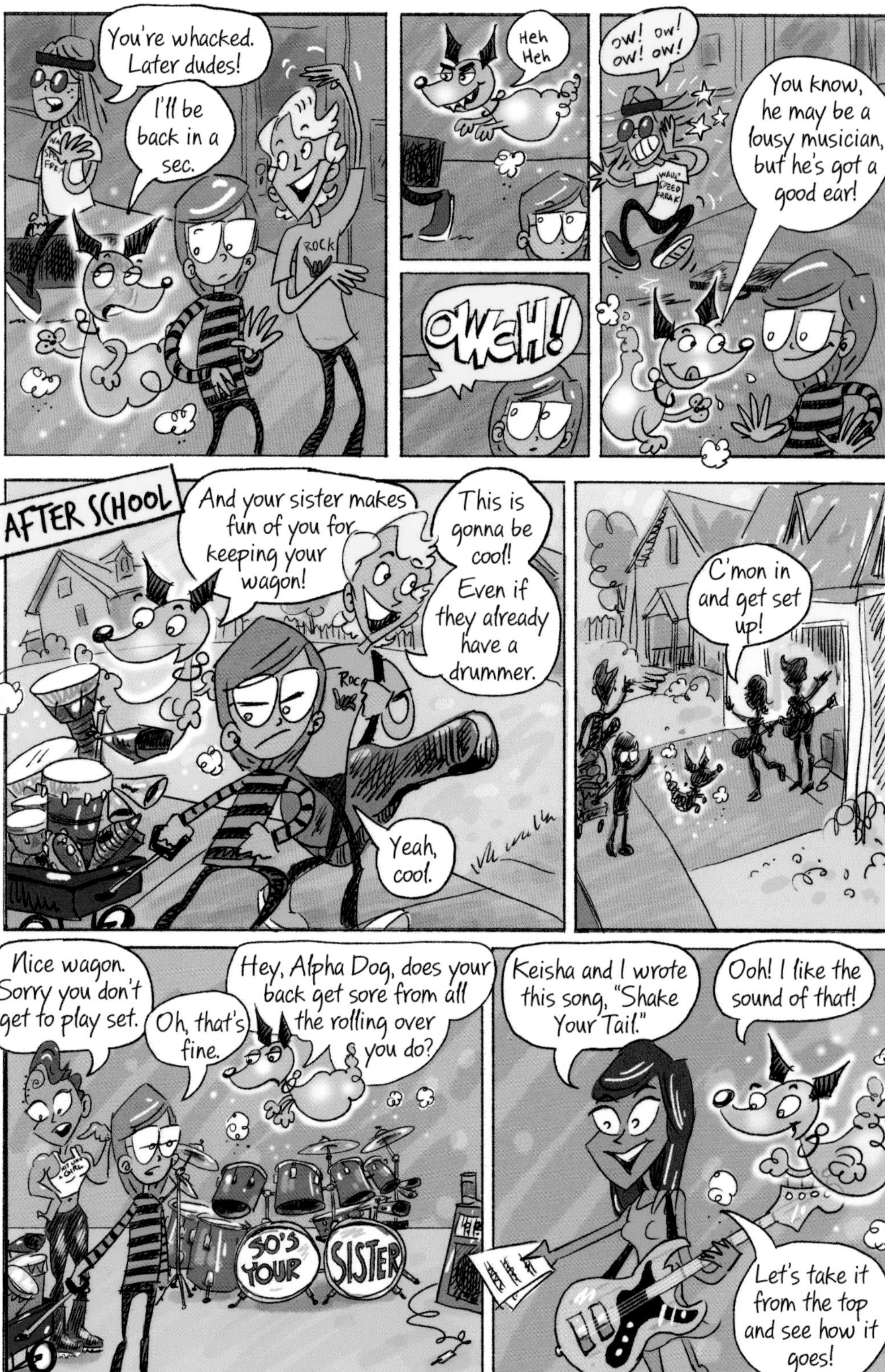
You're whacked. Later dudes!
I'll be back in a sec.
Heh Heh
OW! OW! OW! OW!
OWCH!
You know, he may be a lousy musician, but he's got a good ear!
AFTER SCHOOL
And your sister makes fun of you for keeping your wagon!
This is gonna be cool!
Even if they already have a drummer.
Yeah, cool.
C'mon in and get set up!
Nice wagon. Sorry you don't get to play set.
Oh, that's fine.
Hey, Alpha Dog, does your back get sore from all the rolling over you do?
SO'S YOUR SISTER
Keisha and I wrote this song, "Shake Your Tail."
Ooh! I like the sound of that!
Let's take it from the top and see how it goes!

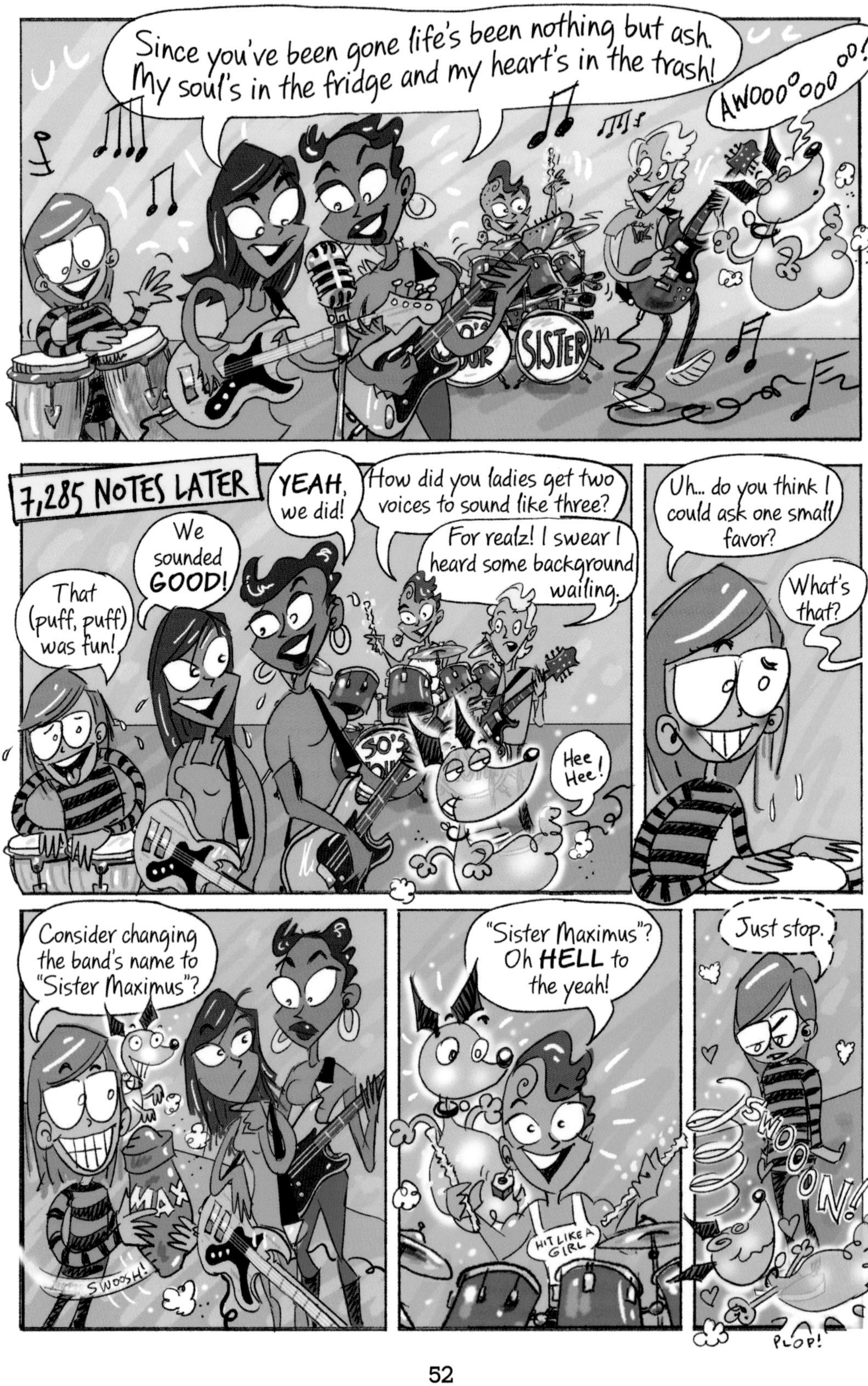
Since you've been gone life's been nothing but ash. My soul's in the fridge and my heart's in the trash!
AWOOOOOOOO!
SISTER
7,285 NOTES LATER
That (puff, puff) was fun!
We sounded **GOOD!**
YEAH, we did!
How did you ladies get two voices to sound like three?
For realz! I swear I heard some background wailing.
Hee Hee!
Uh... do you think I could ask one small favor?
What's that?
Consider changing the band's name to "Sister Maximus"?
MAX
SWOOSH!
"Sister Maximus"? Oh **HELL** to the yeah!
HIT LIKE A GIRL
Just stop.
SWOOOON!
PLOP!

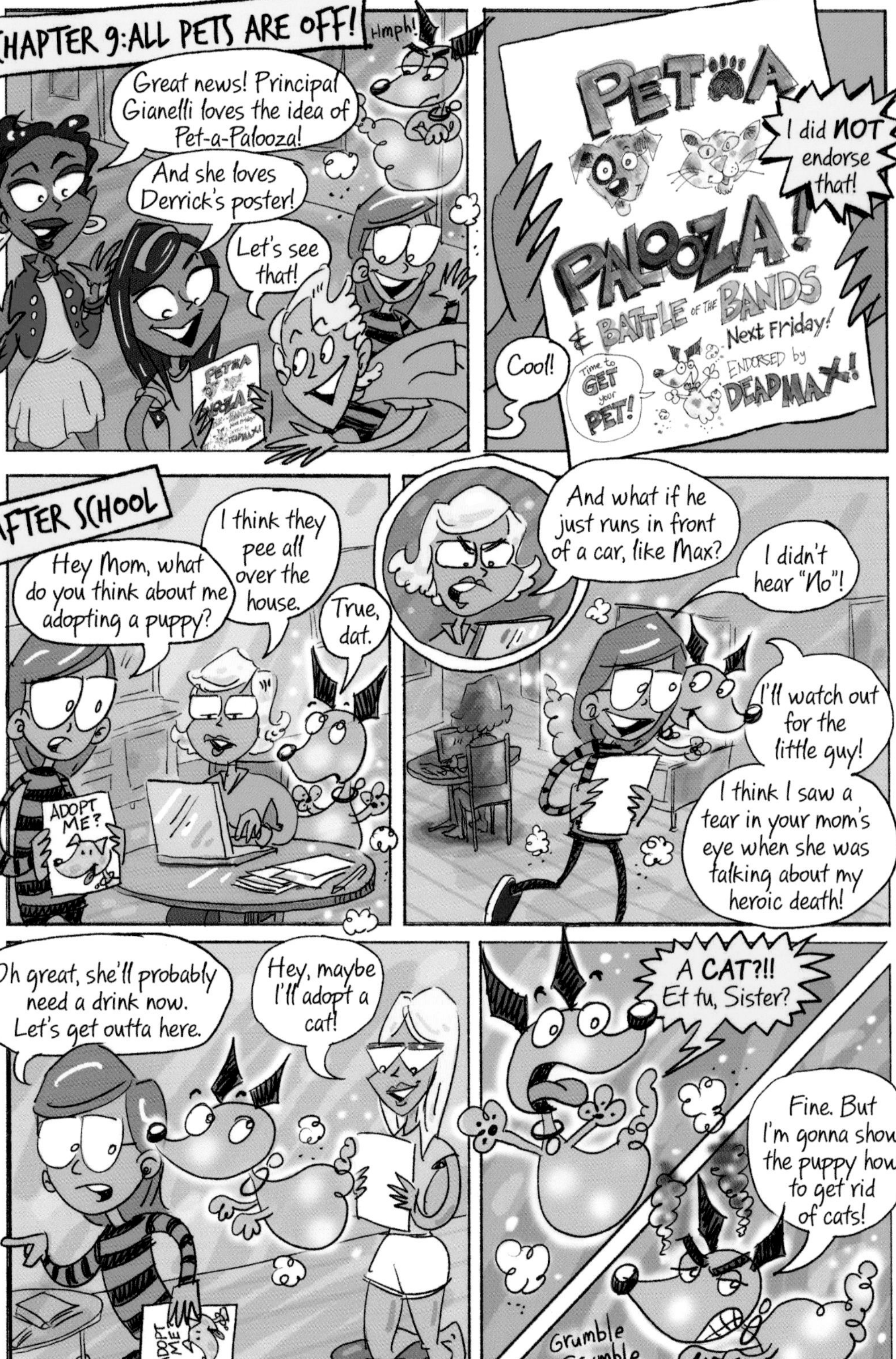
CHAPTER 9: ALL PETS ARE OFF!
Hmph!
Great news! Principal Gianelli loves the idea of Pet-a-Palooza!
And she loves Derrick's poster!
Let's see that!
PET-A-PALOOZA! & BATTLE OF THE BANDS
Next Friday!
Time to GET your PET!
ENDORSED by DEAD MAX!
I did NOT endorse that!
Cool!
AFTER SCHOOL
Hey Mom, what do you think about me adopting a puppy?
I think they pee all over the house.
True, dat.
ADOPT ME?
And what if he just runs in front of a car, like Max?
I didn't hear "No"!
I'll watch out for the little guy!
I think I saw a tear in your mom's eye when she was talking about my heroic death!
Oh great, she'll probably need a drink now. Let's get outta here.
Hey, maybe I'll adopt a cat!
ADOPT ME
A CAT?!! Et tu, Sister?
Fine. But I'm gonna show the puppy how to get rid of cats!
Grumble Grumble

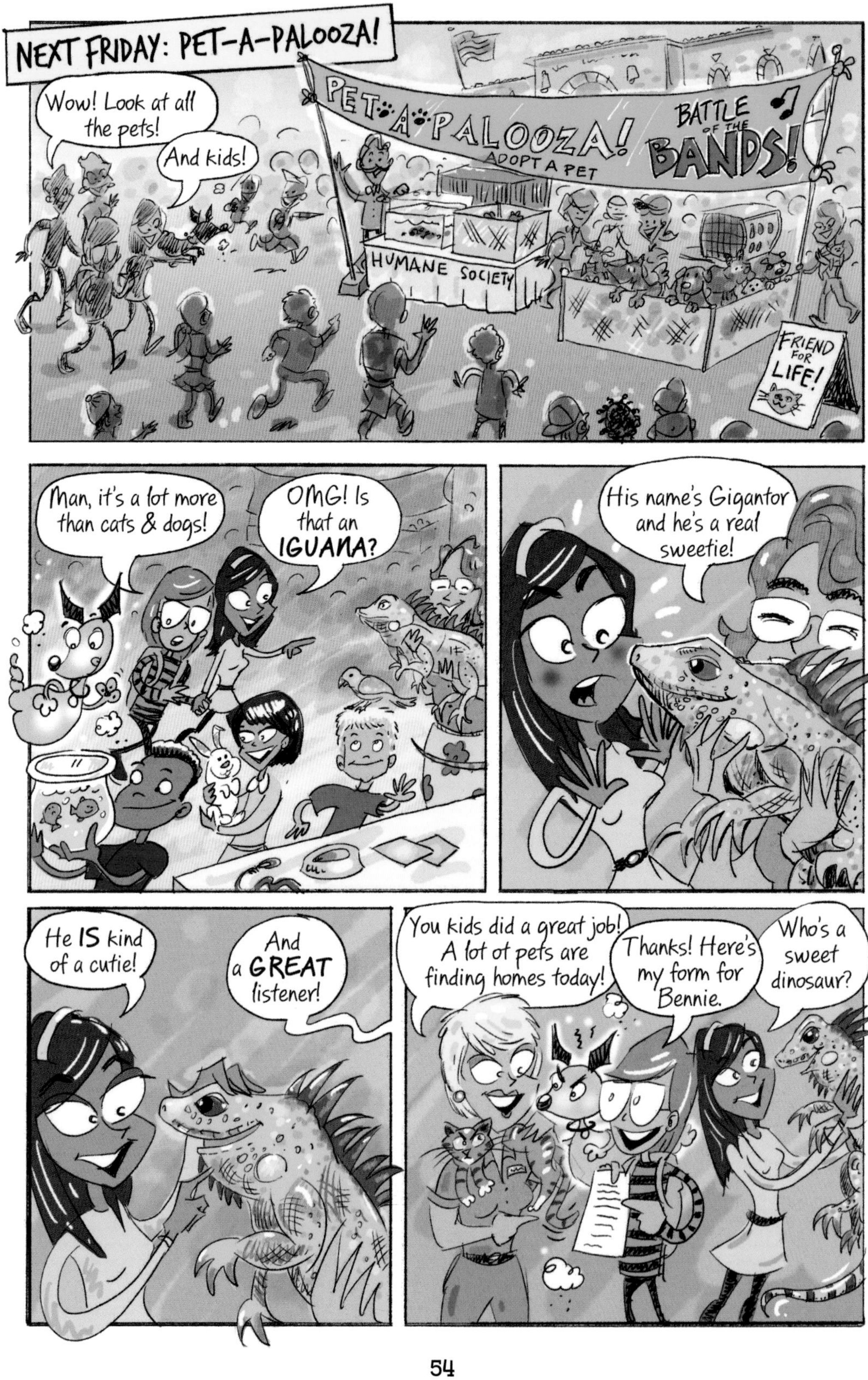
NEXT FRIDAY: PET-A-PALOOZA!
Wow! Look at all the pets!
And kids!
PET-A-PALOOZA!
ADOPT A PET
BATTLE OF THE BANDS!
HUMANE SOCIETY
FRIEND FOR LIFE!
Man, it's a lot more than cats & dogs!
OMG! Is that an IGUANA?
His name's Gigantor and he's a real sweetie!
He IS kind of a cutie!
And a GREAT listener!
You kids did a great job! A lot of pets are finding homes today!
Thanks! Here's my form for Bennie.
Who's a sweet dinosaur?

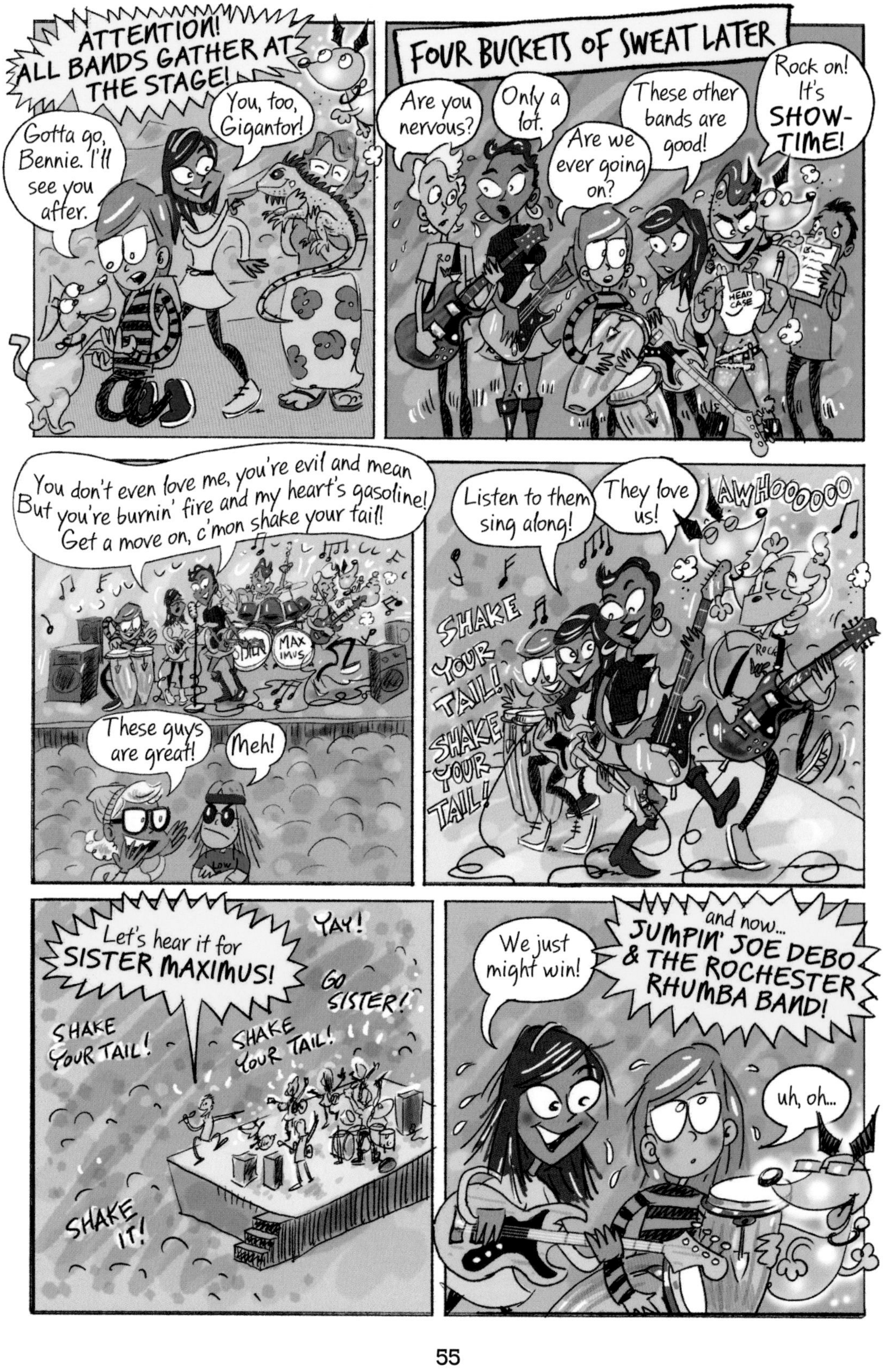
ATTENTION! ALL BANDS GATHER AT THE STAGE!
Gotta go, Bennie. I'll see you after.
You, too, Gigantor!
FOUR BUCKETS OF SWEAT LATER
Are you nervous?
Only a lot.
Are we ever going on?
These other bands are good!
Rock on! It's SHOW-TIME!
HEAD CASE
You don't even love me, you're evil and mean
But you're burnin' fire and my heart's gasoline!
Get a move on, c'mon shake your tail!
MAX IMUS
These guys are great!
Meh!
Listen to them sing along!
They love us!
AWHOOOOOOO
SHAKE YOUR TAIL! SHAKE YOUR TAIL!
Let's hear it for SISTER MAXIMUS!
YAY!
GO SISTER!
SHAKE YOUR TAIL!
SHAKE YOUR TAIL!
SHAKE IT!
We just might win!
and now... JUMPIN' JOE DEBO & THE ROCHESTER RHUMBA BAND!
uh, oh...

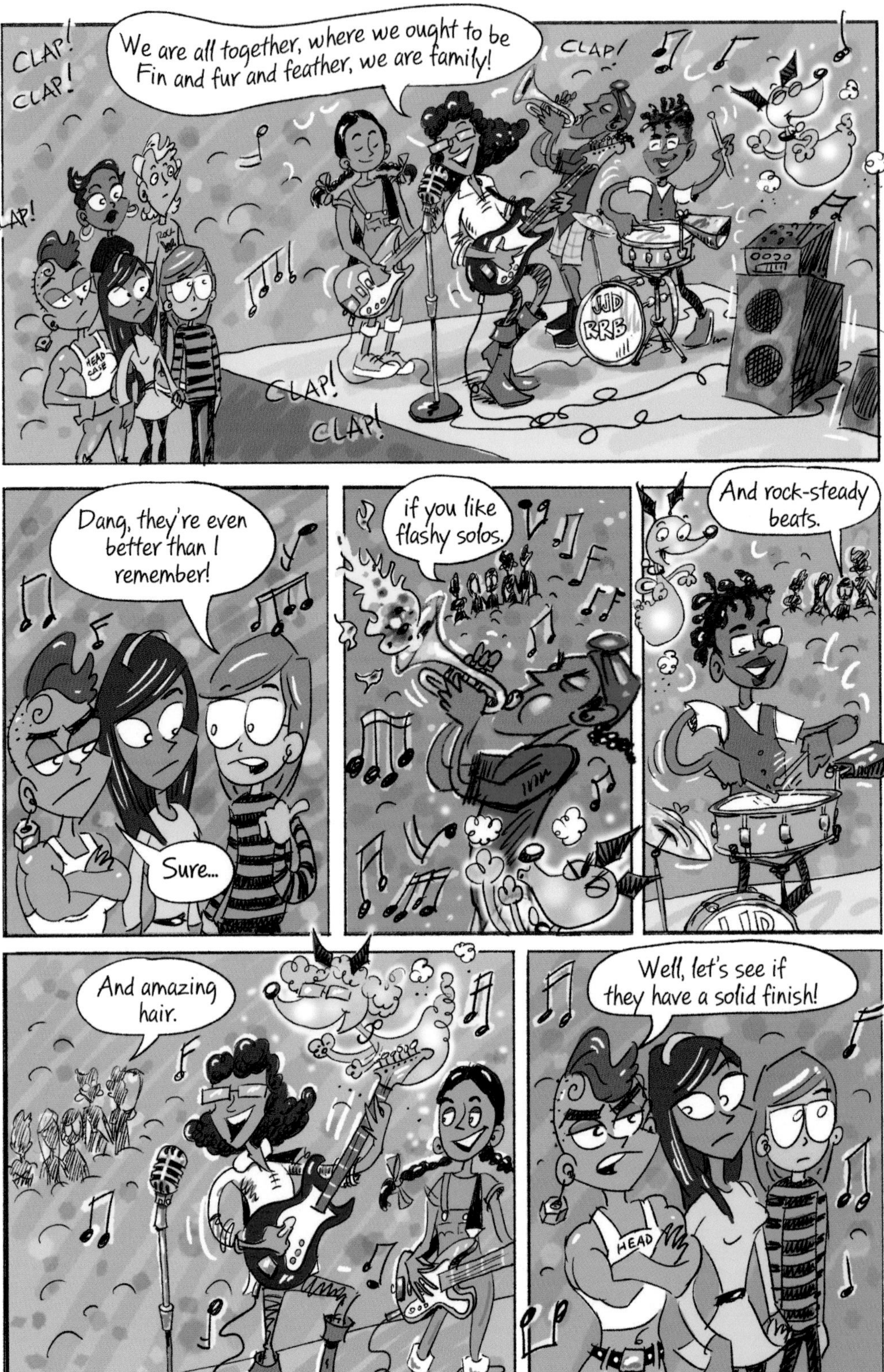
CLAP! CLAP!
We are all together, where we ought to be
Fin and fur and feather, we are family!
CLAP!
CLAP!
CLAP!
CLAP!
JJD RRB
Dang, they're even better than I remember!
Sure...
if you like flashy solos.
And rock-steady beats.
And amazing hair.
Well, let's see if they have a solid finish!
HEAD

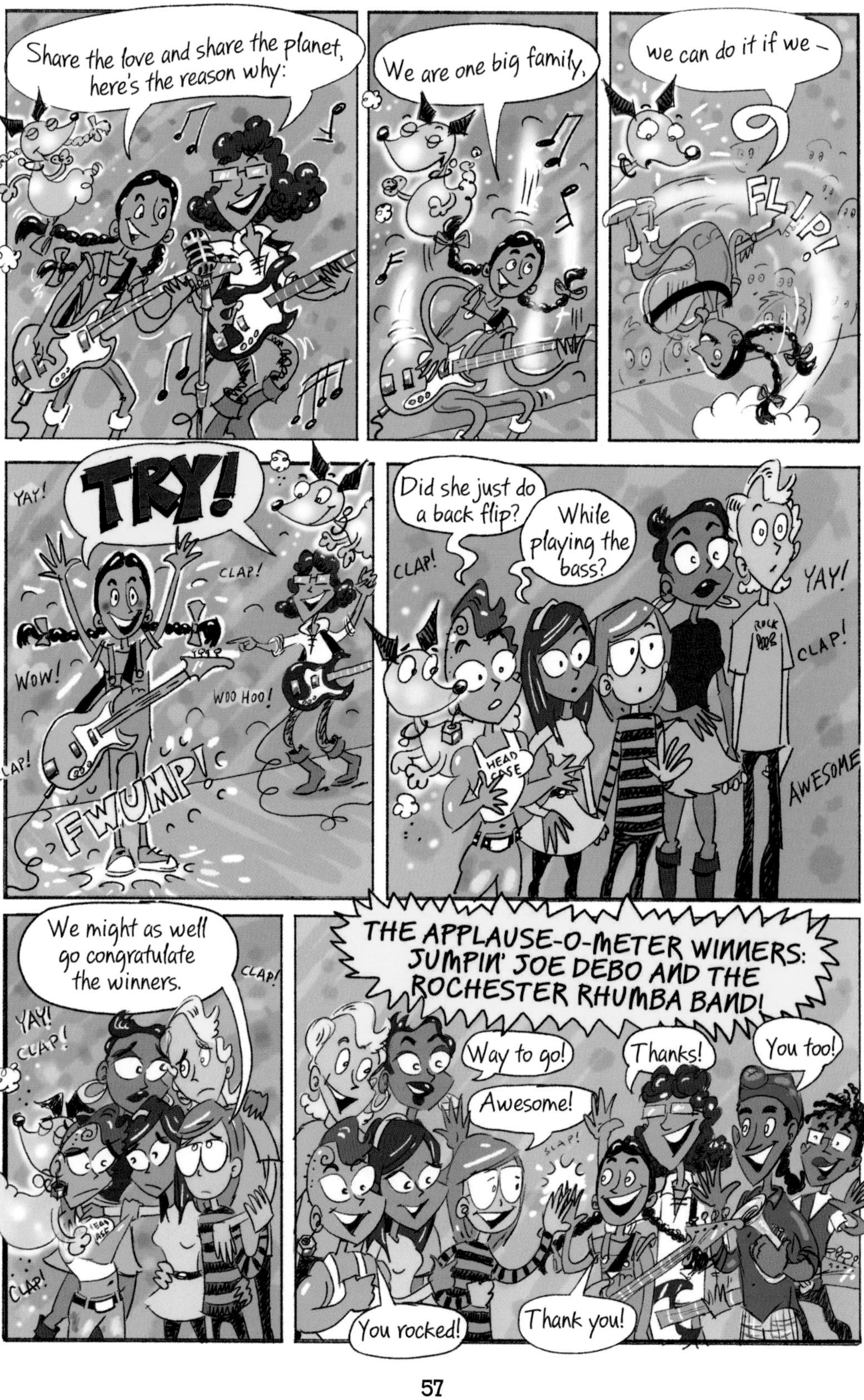
Share the love and share the planet, here's the reason why:
We are one big family,
we can do it if we –
FLIP!
TRY!
YAY!
CLAP!
WOW!
WOO HOO!
CLAP!
FWUMP!
Did she just do a back flip?
While playing the bass?
CLAP!
YAY!
CLAP!
HEAD CASE
AWESOME!
We might as well go congratulate the winners.
CLAP!
YAY!
CLAP!
CLAP!
THE APPLAUSE-O-METER WINNERS: JUMPIN' JOE DEBO AND THE ROCHESTER RHUMBA BAND!
Way to go!
Thanks!
You too!
Awesome!
You rocked!
Thank you!

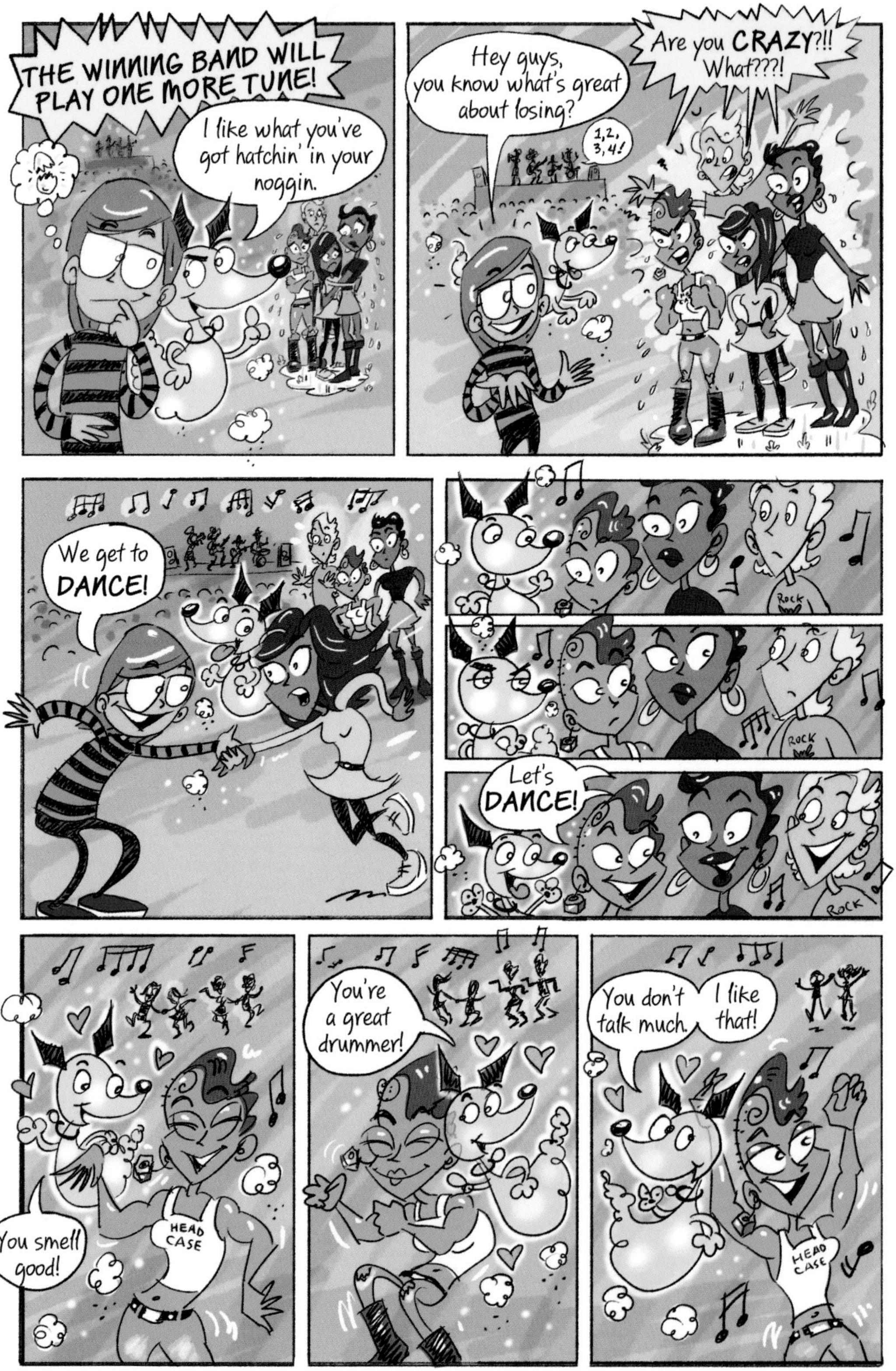
THE WINNING BAND WILL PLAY ONE MORE TUNE!
I like what you've got hatchin' in your noggin.
Hey guys, you know what's great about losing?
1, 2, 3, 4!
Are you CRAZY?!! What???!
We get to DANCE!
Let's DANCE!
ROCK
You smell good!
HEAD CASE
You're a great drummer!
You don't talk much.
I like that!

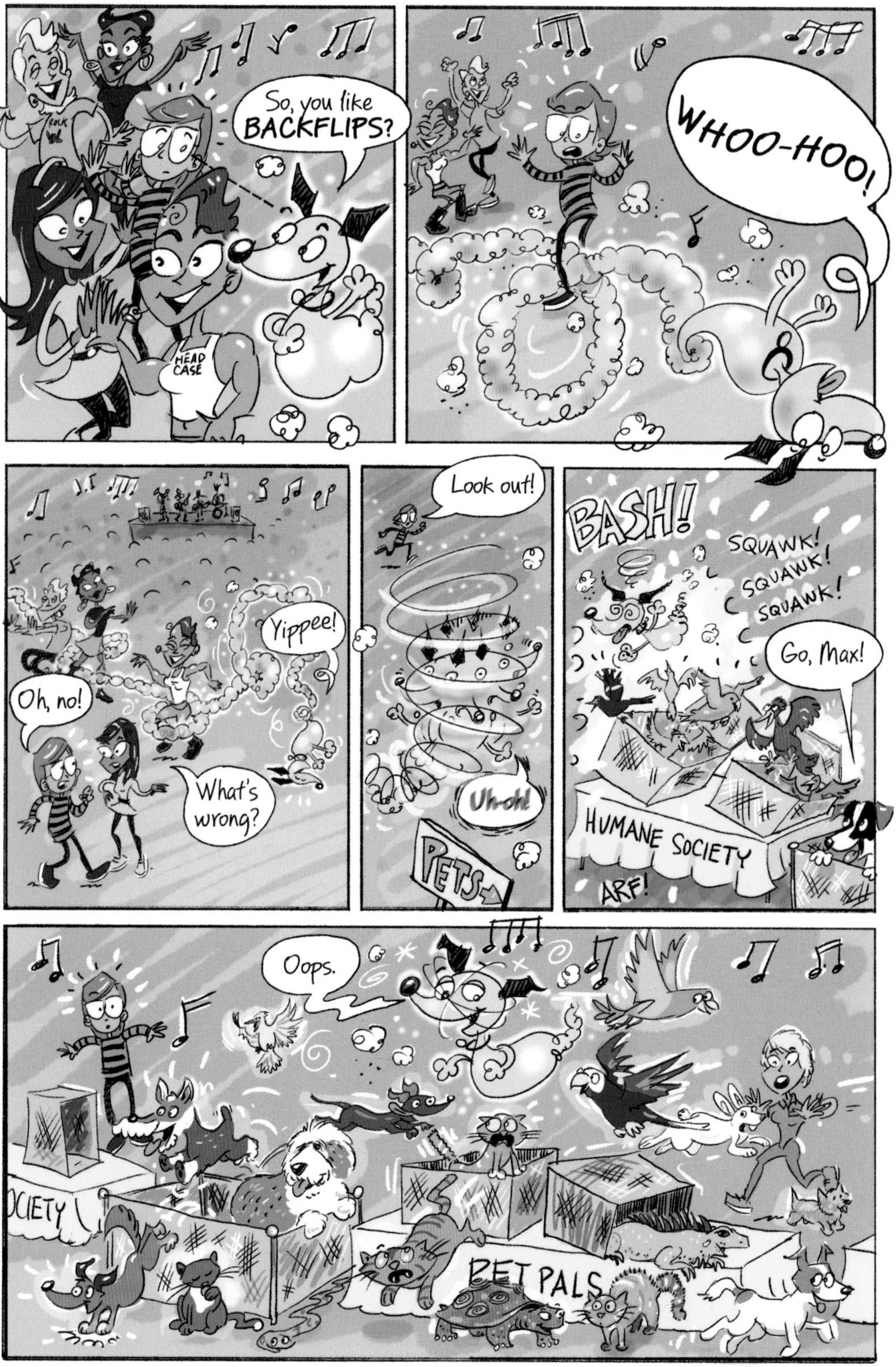
So, you like BACKFLIPS?
WHOO-HOO!
Oh, no!
Yippee!
What's wrong?
Look out!
Uh-oh!
PETS
BASH!
SQUAWK! SQUAWK! SQUAWK!
Go, Max!
HUMANE SOCIETY
ARF!
Oops.
OCIETY
PET PALS

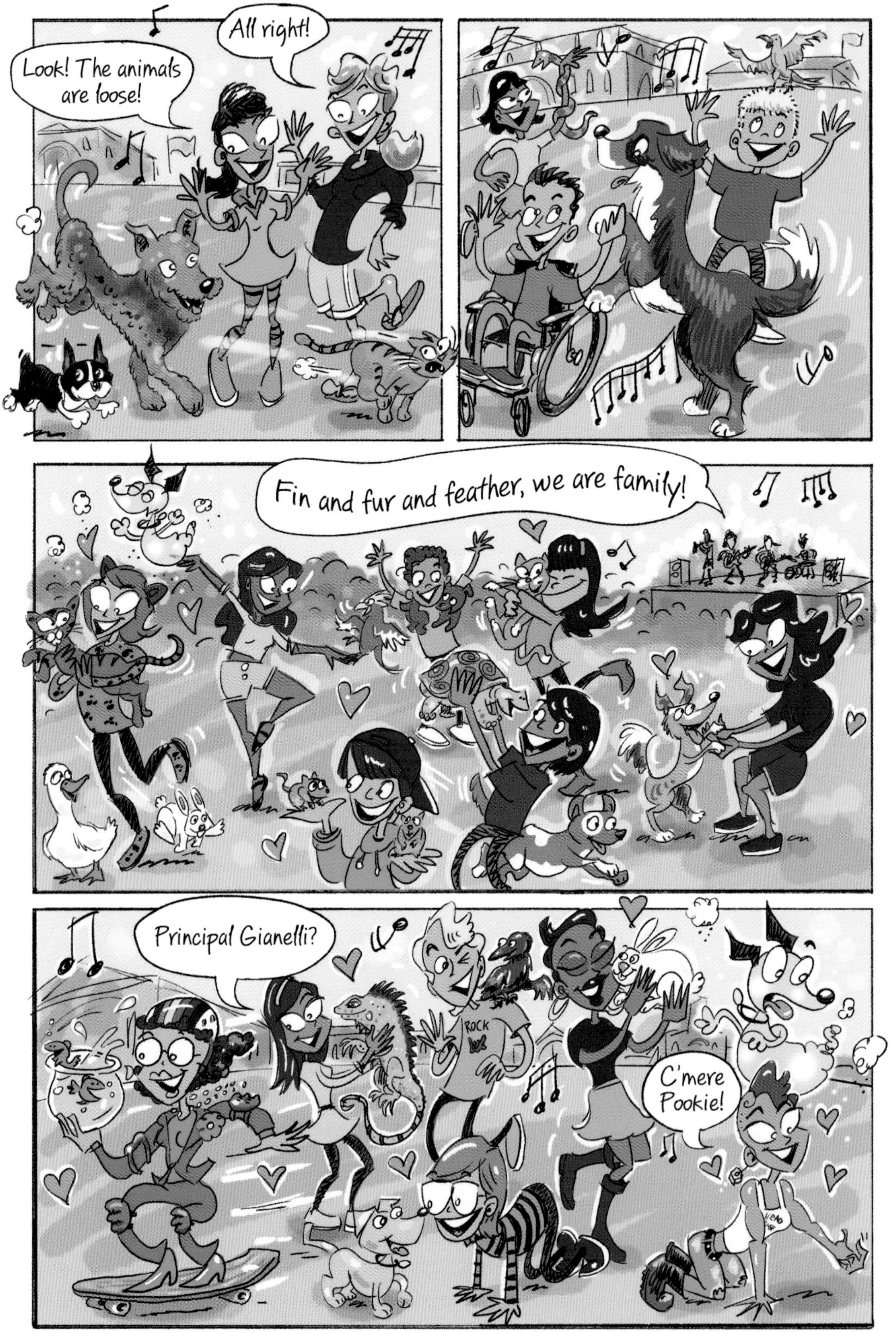
Look! The animals are loose!
All right!
Fin and fur and feather, we are family!
Principal Gianelli?
ROCK
C'mere Pookie!

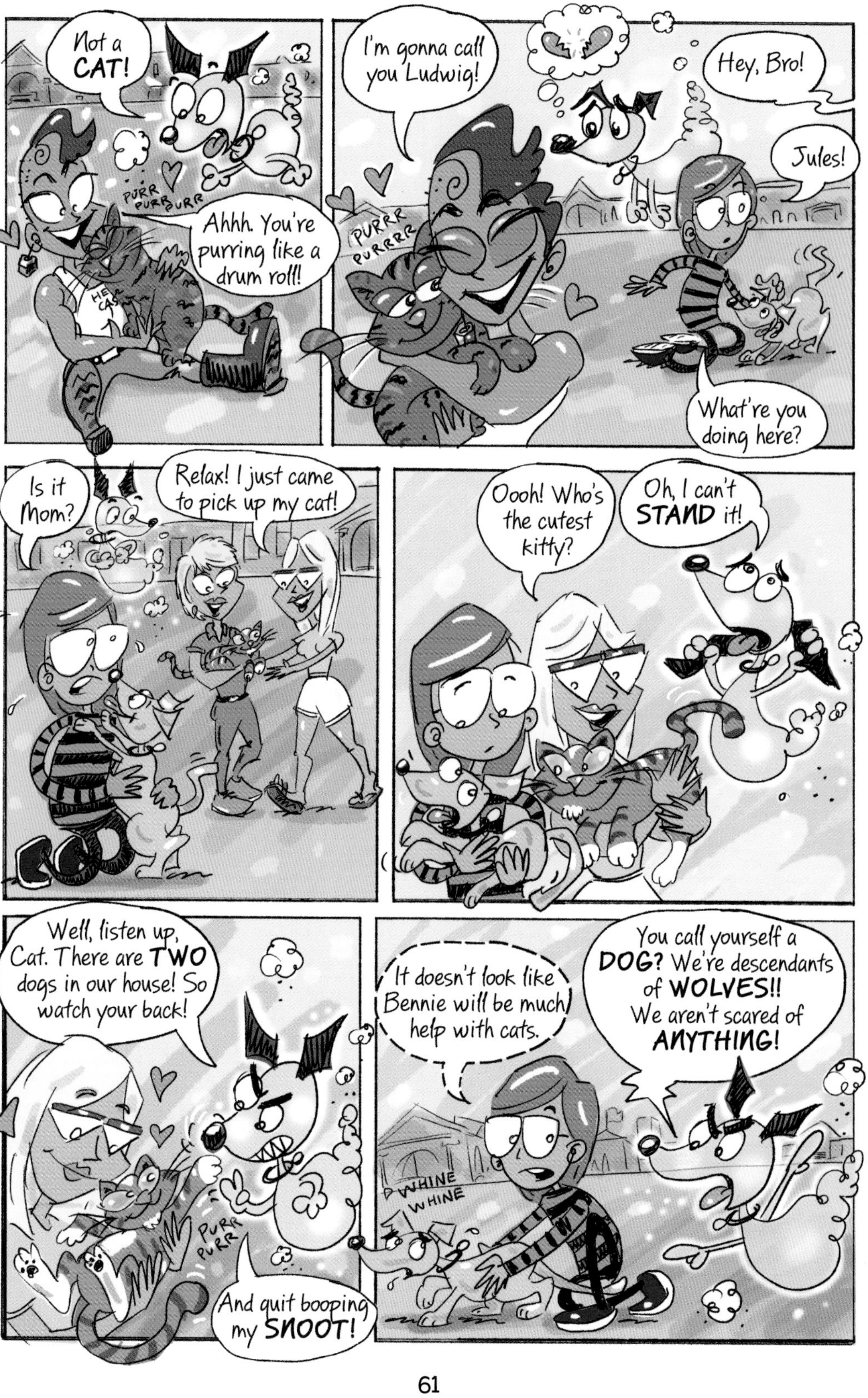
Not a CAT!
PURR PURR PURR
Ahhh. You're purring like a drum roll!
I'm gonna call you Ludwig!
PURRR PURRRR
Hey, Bro!
Jules!
What're you doing here?
Is it Mom?
Relax! I just came to pick up my cat!
Oooh! Who's the cutest kitty?
Oh, I can't STAND it!
Well, listen up, Cat. There are TWO dogs in our house! So watch your back!
PURR PURR
And quit booping my SNOOT!
It doesn't look like Bennie will be much help with cats.
You call yourself a DOG? We're descendants of WOLVES!! We aren't scared of ANYTHING!
WHINE WHINE

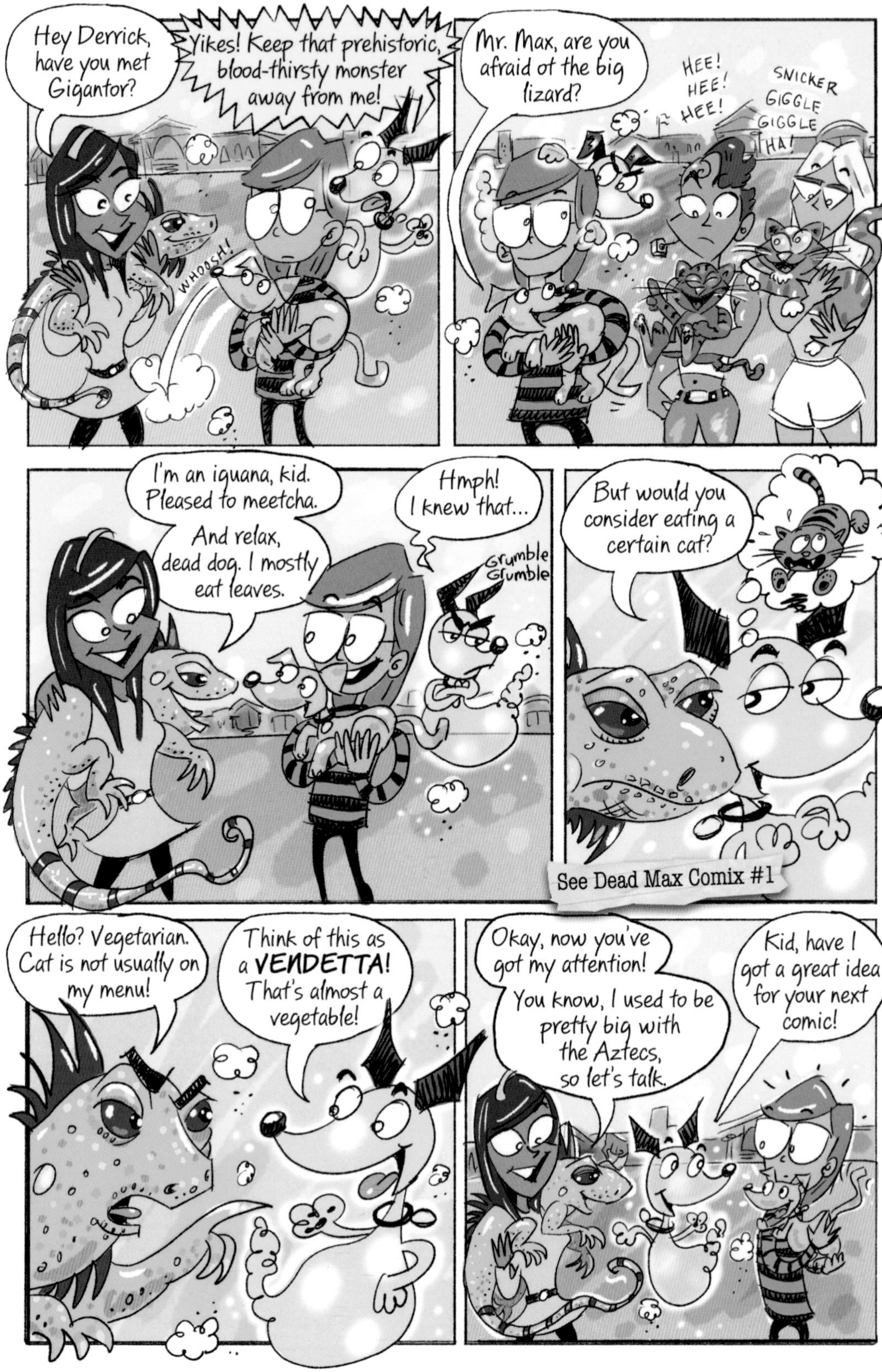

Hey Derrick, have you met Gigantor?
Yikes! Keep that prehistoric, blood-thirsty monster away from me!
WHOOSH!
Mr. Max, are you afraid of the big lizard?
HEE! HEE! HEE!
SNICKER GIGGLE GIGGLE HA!
I'm an iguana, kid. Pleased to meetcha.
And relax, dead dog. I mostly eat leaves.
Hmph! I knew that...
Grumble Grumble
But would you consider eating a certain cat?
See Dead Max Comix #1
Hello? Vegetarian. Cat is not usually on my menu!
Think of this as a **VENDETTA**! That's almost a vegetable!
Okay, now you've got my attention!
You know, I used to be pretty big with the Aztecs, so let's talk.
Kid, have I got a great idea for your next comic!

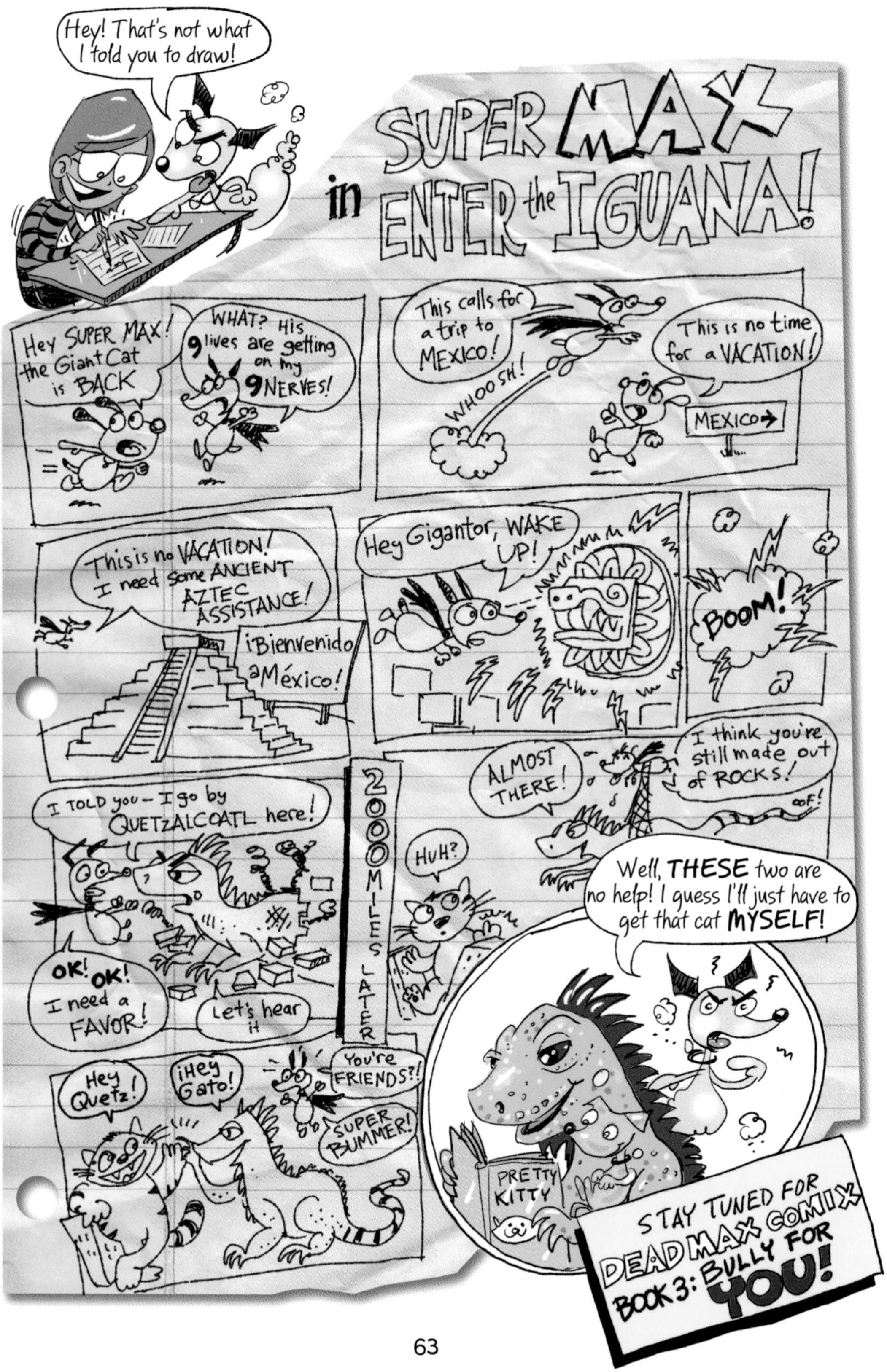

Hey! That's not what I told you to draw!
SUPER MAX in ENTER the IGUANA!
Hey SUPER MAX! the Giant Cat is BACK
WHAT? His 9 lives are getting on my 9 NERVES!
This calls for a trip to MEXICO!
WHOOSH!
This is no time for a VACATION!
MEXICO
This is no VACATION! I need some ANCIENT AZTEC ASSISTANCE!
¡Bienvenido a México!
Hey Gigantor, WAKE UP!
BOOM!
I TOLD you – I go by QUETZALCOATL here!
OK! OK! I need a FAVOR!
Let's hear it
2000 MILES LATER
HUH?
ALMOST THERE!
I think you're still made out of ROCKS!
OOF!
Hey Quetz!
¡Hey Gato!
You're FRIENDS?!
SUPER BUMMER!
Well, THESE two are no help! I guess I'll just have to get that cat MYSELF!
PRETTY KITTY
STAY TUNED FOR DEAD MAX COMIX BOOK 3: BULLY FOR YOU!

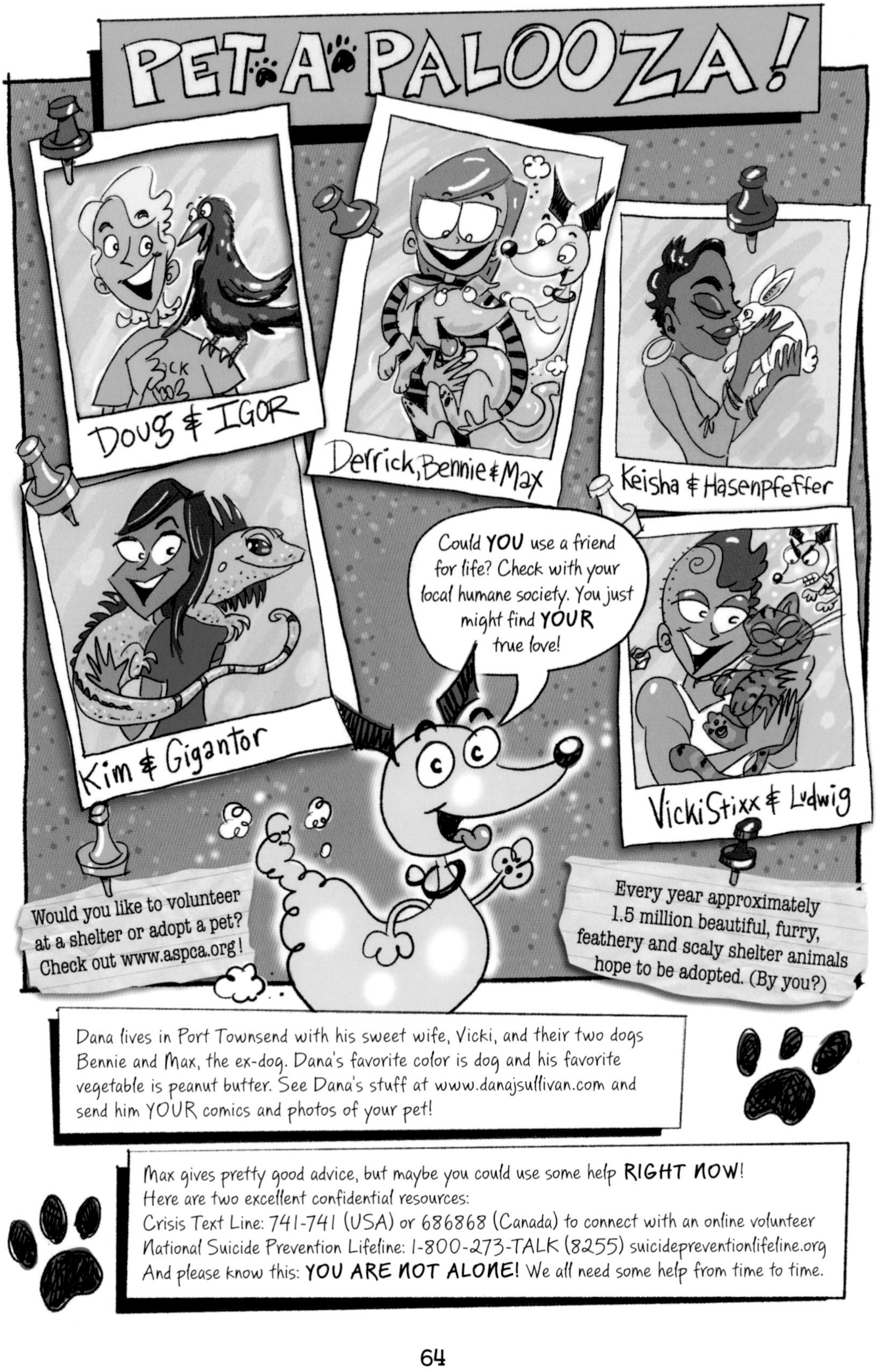
PET-A-PALOOZA!
Doug & IGOR
Derrick, Bennie & Max
Keisha & Hasenpfeffer
Kim & Gigantor
Could YOU use a friend for life? Check with your local humane society. You just might find YOUR true love!
VickiStixx & Ludwig
Would you like to volunteer at a shelter or adopt a pet? Check out www.aspca.org!
Every year approximately 1.5 million beautiful, furry, feathery and scaly shelter animals hope to be adopted. (By you?)

Dana lives in Port Townsend with his sweet wife, Vicki, and their two dogs Bennie and Max, the ex-dog. Dana's favorite color is dog and his favorite vegetable is peanut butter. See Dana's stuff at www.danajsullivan.com and send him YOUR comics and photos of your pet!

Max gives pretty good advice, but maybe you could use some help **RIGHT NOW**!
Here are two excellent confidential resources:
Crisis Text Line: 741-741 (USA) or 686868 (Canada) to connect with an online volunteer
National Suicide Prevention Lifeline: 1-800-273-TALK (8255) suicidepreventionlifeline.org
And please know this: **YOU ARE NOT ALONE!** We all need some help from time to time.